I0847379

# FINDING JONAH

## A SWEET INSPIRATIONAL BROTHER'S BEST FRIEND ROMANCE

### BEACON BLUFF SERIES
### BOOK ONE

## DENISE GORE LONG

Copyright © 2025 by Denise Gore Long

All rights reserved.

No part of this book may be reproduced in any form or by any electronic or mechanical means, including information storage and retrieval systems, without written permission from the author, except for the use of brief quotations in a book review.

Cover Design: Cindy Beyer

Editors: Rona Gofstein and Sara Turnquist

Proofreading: Cindy Beyer

*This book is dedicated to Miss Mona Ballard,
my high school English teacher—
who, somehow, saw something in me worth encouraging.*

# CHAPTER 1

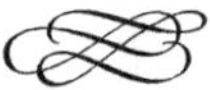

The day her husband died had also been the day Arden Gray began to live.

One year ago, she had stood in a hospital room, drowning in grief and disbelief. Today, she stood on a breezy coastline, inhaling the salt air as if it were her fresh start.

The early morning beach was hers alone, save a lone jogger approaching in the distance. Her steps fell in rhythm with the runner's bobbing neon orange baseball cap. Even the early-bird treasure hunters hadn't made an appearance. Too bad. The storm would have coughed up all sorts of treasures onto the North Carolina shore. The lapping surf kissed Arden's shoes as she dodged driftwood, broken seashells, and piles of seaweed.

A clump of something tumbling in the tide caught her eye. It seemed out of place among the other storm surge debris. Sure enough, the clouds parted, and sunlight revealed an animal's struggle to keep its head above water.

The muddy bundle rolled in the breaker, and she rushed in. A wave crashed into her above her knees, impeding her progress. She gasped, gritted her teeth against the frigid water, and pressed on.

The surf spit the bundle into her arms. She now held a limp, barely breathing dog. Its head lolled over her forearm, mouth opening and closing as if it were trying to speak. A choking sound escaped, but he lacked the strength to do anything but quiver.

Arden turned and allowed the tide to push her toward shore. Stumbling onto firm sand, her sobs were drowned out by the ocean's roar. She dropped to her knees and laid the dog in the sand. *Please Lord! Help me!*

No time to Google dog CPR. So instead, she flashed back to her babysitting days. The mouth. Check the airway.

The poor baby was so out of it, his self-protective instincts were non-existent. He let Arden sweep her finger across his tongue. Good. No obstruction.

His chest heaved with shallow gasps. CPR wouldn't be needed after all. At least, for now. What should she do next?

The pup lay limp on the beach, energy waning before her eyes. Matted fur had turned ashen from caked layers of sand. Even soaked, he couldn't weigh much more than a hunk of driftwood. Skin sunk between each rib as his chest rose and fell in an uneven rhythm.

A deep ache in those brown eyes tugged at her chest.

She bit her lip and swallowed another sob. She couldn't help him if she didn't get a grip. "I've got you. Don't you worry."

There were several scratches on his belly, one deeper than the rest and bleeding. Pulling off her fabric headband, she cautiously wrapped it around the dog's midsection to stem the blood flow.

A vet. The dog needed a vet.

Trying not to jostle him, she gathered him close.

Arden hadn't succeeded in marriage. She hadn't saved her husband, but she would save this animal. Nothing else would perish on her watch.

Her wet sneakers sucked the loose sand. A stumble nearly sent her—and the tiny dog—tumbling, but a steady hand caught her just in time.

Startled, she cried out and stumbled, clutching the dog. There'd been no sound, no warning—just a presence at her side.

The runner, catching his breath, focused on the dog in her arms. "Let me see." He reached out, but Arden pulled back.

"No. I've got to get him to a vet."

"I am a vet." His forceful tone brought her up short. "Now please, let me see."

This wasn't the time to ask for credentials or bristle at his high-handed attitude. She had to believe God had delivered a veterinarian angel sporting an orange cap.

"Save him." Arden thrust the animal into his arms.

The stranger gently laid the pup in the sand, every movement urgent and precise.

She prayed as she sank to her knees, grateful for the man's sure hands as they moved along the dog's body.

His lips pressed into a thin line. "He's taken in a lot of water. He's suffocating."

Her throat closed. "Drowning? What can we do? Let me help."

The man picked up the dog and turned him upside down.

Arden gasped as he held him by his back legs and gently swung him from side to side. "What are you doing?"

Could this man really be a vet? Maybe she should have asked for proof after all.

Frothy water trickled from the dog's mouth, the gagging sound both scary and encouraging.

Okay. Maybe Dr. Vet did know what he was doing.

Out of the corner of her eye, Arden spotted a woman about twenty paces away with three leashed dogs scrambling at her feet. At least she wasn't interfering.

When the water stopped dribbling from the dog's mouth, the vet rolled him onto his back and placed two fingers against his chest. Every careful touch reassured Arden that he knew exactly what he was doing.

Putting his ear close to the dog's body, Dr. Vet sighed. "Thank God. There's a heartbeat, but he's still struggling to breathe. I need to get him to the clinic. Now."

"I'll call Dr. Weston," she said, digging out her phone. Beacon Bluff's vet wouldn't be open yet, but his answering service would alert him to the emergency. "I'm sure he'll meet us there."

"No need. I have the key." He flung the words over his shoulder, his long legs already eating up the sand.

Not questioning why this stranger would have a key to the local veterinarian clinic, Arden turned to follow. A quick glance revealed the other woman was filming them with her phone. Arden frowned. Was she seriously filming this?

There was no time to hesitate—she charged up the stairs, the pup's protector already forging ahead. "I'll drive so you can hold him. My car's not far."

He nodded, silently requesting for her to lead the way, his eyes never leaving his patient.

She jogged to stay ahead of his long strides. "This way."

They reached her SUV. Arden never locked its doors and stored the key in the console—a benefit of living in Beacon Bluff during off season. She punched the button to start the engine.

"Crank up the heat. He's showing signs of hypothermia."

A quick glance at the dog revealed a violent tremble shaking his small frame. No argument—just a quick reach into the backseat for a spare sweatshirt. "Here, wrap him in this."

With a quick shift into reverse, the tires kicked up gravel as the car shot backward. *Lord, please let us make it to the clinic in time.*

*L*ORD, *please let us make it to the clinic in one piece.*

Blondie tore down the two-lane rural road, white-knuckling the steering wheel.

Nick cradled the dog in his lap, his fingers pressed against its chest, feeling for the faint heartbeat.

She stomped on the brake and the SUV lurched to a stop in front of the clinic. Fortunately, there weren't many pedestrians this time of morning, so there were no casualties from her adrenaline-fueled driving.

The clinic door flew open before they could exit the vehicle. Stella Carter, the clinic's vet tech, had clearly spotted them coming. She rushed ahead, flicking on lights and opening doors.

Blondie trailed behind, her anxiety a palpable force driving him forward.

Nick focused on the small patient now lying on the stainless-steel exam table. No wasting words. No hesitation. "Pulmonary edema. Oxygen, IV port, warm saline." His heart pounded. At the edge of his vision, Blondie stood frozen, wide-eyed.

Stella moved with controlled speed, cutting away the makeshift tourniquet and setting up the life-saving equipment. Bandages, injections, an oxygen mask. The hum of equipment filled the room.

Then...stillness.

Nick's breath hitched. No gasping. No chest movement.

"No heartbeat." His voice sliced through the quiet.

He glanced over his shoulder. Blondie was hunched against the wall, resting on her head in her hands.

His heart squeezed, but there was no time for soft feelings. "Blondie, I need you here. Hold his head steady. Stella, remove the mask and prep epinephrine."

Both women sprang into action. Blondie cradled the dog's head—not too tight, not too gentle.

Nick placed his hands over the animal's chest. "Starting compressions." His voice became the metronome. "One, two, three, four..."

Each tick of the clock pulsed through his body. The oxygen machine hissed in the background.

"Fifteen." He tilted the dog's head back and gave two life-saving breaths.

The dog's chest rose and fell, then stilled.

"Come on, buddy, don't give up," Nick muttered, resuming compressions. "Stella. Epinephrine. Now."

She injected the medication.

They watched. They waited.

Nick resumed compressions, aware of Blondie's quiet sniffs. He didn't need to look—tears were no doubt traveling down her cheeks.

"Thirty." Another cycle. Another two breaths. Then...a weak cough

Nick exhaled, his muscles loosened, and the adrenaline began to ebb.

"Is he breathing?" Blondie's voice broke, raw with hope.

He pressed two fingers to the tiny chest. "We have a heart-beat." His smile stretched across his face, showcasing his profound sense of relief. For the first time in a long time, his eyes burned with something more than exhaustion. This is what he'd trained for.

Nick took Blondie's hand and placed it beneath his own against the animal's side, experiencing together the faint but steady thump of life. Her smile lit up the room like a beacon in the storm.

Nick pulled back. The moment blurred the line between professional detachment and something far more dangerous. They'd bonded after sharing an intense rescue. That's all this was.

He cleared his throat. "It's okay to pet him. He may enjoy hearing your voice."

Blondie kissed the dog's head and caressed his front paw. "Hello, sweetheart. Feeling better?"

The pup blinked and his tail gave the faintest quiver—not a wag, but something.

Nick watched as she took in the dog's filthy fur, tangled with seaweed and brambles.

The pup reeked of seaweed and decay, but she didn't seem to care. She rested her cheek against his head and something in Nick's throat tightened.

"He's a dachshund, right?" Her voice was thick with emotion. "How old do you think he is?"

Nick lifted the pup's lip. "Yes. Long-haired, red variety. He appears fully grown. My guess? Around two years old, but he's severely underweight so it's hard to tell. Any idea where he came from?"

"No." She rested a hand on the dachshund's chest. "It's okay, little one. You're safe now."

Nick would bet his last vintage t-shirt that this dog had tumbled into his forever home. "Maybe he fell off a boat during last night's storm. Or fell in by the rocks."

"I can't imagine." She blinked hard to keep tears at bay.

"Hey, it's okay. He's beaten the odds so far." Nick placed a reassuring hand on her shoulder and handed her a tissue.

The warmth beneath her hoodie took the chill from his fingers.

His touch seemed to break the dam. Her emotions flooded her eyes and, though she tried, her lips couldn't contain her sobs. She pinched the bridge of her nose, struggling for breath.

No guy wanted to deal with a strange woman's ugly cry, but somehow, he didn't mind. Not with this woman.

Gulping, she sniffed and waved her hand. "Don't mind me. Long night. No sleep."

He chuckled and bent to catch her lowered gaze. "Come here." He hooked his arm around her shoulders for a side hug.

She leaned in, and he stood steady as floodgates opened and

waterworks flowed. Would it hurt to let her rest her head, just for a moment?

The exam room door burst open.

Blondie flinched and jerked away from him. She swiped at her cheeks as if erasing all evidence of her breakdown. She straightened, rolling her shoulders back as if bracing for battle.

A woman stood in the doorway, taking them both in, her shrewd gaze not missing a beat. She strode forward, hand extended. "Tiffany Meyers. Coastal Cable News."

Blondie crossed her arms, ignoring the handshake. "You're kidding."

Tiffany didn't blink. "I saw the rescue this morning and I'd love to do a human-interest piece for my network. It's classic feel-good stuff."

"How dare you." Blondie's voice was low and dangerous. "For all you know that little guy didn't make it. This man and his tech are trying to save a dog's life, and you want to turn it into entertainment? If you want to take up his time with talk, make an appointment!"

Nick blinked. Where had this spitfire been five minutes ago?

He glanced between the two women.

The reporter's long brown hair was pulled into a sleek ponytail. Blondie's stained leggings and faded hoodie suggested she was about to paint a room or two, but the reporter's athleisure wear suggested she was about to enter a Hollywood yoga studio.

Logic said the reporter was the more conventionally attractive, but as far as he was concerned, logic was overrated.

Tiffany exhaled. "Fine. I'll go, but I'll be in touch." She glanced between them, her smile turning knowing. "Cute couple. Cute dog. It's television gold."

Nick did a mental double-take.

Blondie's jaw about hit the floor. "We're not a couple."

Tiffany just winked. "If you say so." Then, with the air of a woman who always got the last word, she turned and disappeared through the door.

Stella poked her head in from the back, clearly guilty. "Sorry. In the heat of the moment, I must have forgotten to lock the front door." She winced. "I'll take care of it now."

Blondie rubbed her temples. "Unbelievable."

Nick smothered a chuckle. He liked her all riled up. He checked the table to ensure the commotion hadn't disturbed the patient.

Still resting. Good.

Stella returned, shoving a handful of clothing into Blondie's arms. "Here, these should fit. I'm sure you want to get out of those wet clothes."

Blondie eyed the pile—a pepto-pink scrub top, hospital-green scrub pants and white athletic socks. "And I thought you liked me, Stella." She lifted the lime-green Crocs by two fingers.

Nick laughed.

Stella grinned. "It beats sitting around in damp clothes."

Blondie sighed. "Fine. But I'm burning these shoes when I get home." She smiled at Stella. "Thank you, it really will be great to get into dry clothes."

Nick's stomach growled. "Apparently saving lives makes me hungry. Why don't you change, and we'll head across the street for breakfast?" He glanced at his own outfit—a faded Liberty University t-shirt and track pants. "We'll make quite the pair."

She shook her head and avoided his gaze. "No thanks. I'm good."

He tilted his head. What happened to the spitfire? Instead, she looked...smaller. Guarded. Woman, thy name is Rubik's Cube.

He dragged a hand through his hair. "Look, I'm starving. I bet you haven't eaten either." He gave her a half grin. "It's because I haven't showered after my run, isn't it?"

A ghost of a smile flickered, but she still wouldn't meet his eyes.

He expected another refusal.

"Well, I guess I should at least give you a ride back to the beach. And breakfast is the least I can do to thank you." With that said, she escaped into the bathroom then reappeared in all her mismatched glory.

He hid a smile behind a cough.

Chewing her lower lip, she glanced toward the table. "It's okay to leave him?"

"Stella would prefer me out of her way while she cleans him up. She'll monitor him closely. We won't be far."

Before leaving, she planted one last kiss on her furry friend's head.

Nick noticed how her touch lingered. Yeah. This little guy wasn't going anywhere.

He followed her out the door, hands in his pockets. How did a woman wearing a faded hoodie and scrubs the color of anti-nausea medication inspire this inexplicable fascination?

He so didn't have time for this.

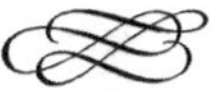

# CHAPTER 2

They crossed the street to the Lamplighter Diner. Like any self-respecting coastal town, Beacon Bluff boasted a narrow main street with pretty shops lined in a row, with colorful awnings paving the way to a postcard-worthy fishing pier.

It always reminded Arden of a Hallmark movie without the snow. Thanks to Hurricane Camilla's visit two years ago, after the repairs the town shimmered like sea glass in the sun—the only bright spot of a devastating event in the town's history.

The economic revival, however, was a different story. Though the town wore its Sunday best, the tourists who once called Beacon Bluff their summer home had migrated to neighboring beach towns.

Maybe it wasn't the ideal time to start a business for vacationers, but Arden hoped her little enterprise might bring people back.

Dr. Vet opened the diner door and motioned for her to go first.

Prickles spread across the back of Arden's neck, ever aware of him behind her. How had she maneuvered herself into breakfast with a man she didn't know? She didn't have the social skills for this.

Arden willed herself not to trip in the oversized Crocs and too-long scrubs, reminding herself that she'd once headed committees full of intimidating women. She could certainly survive breakfast with a kind man who'd saved her dog. Even if he did have serious crush potential.

The diner's exterior had needed serious work after Camilla, but the inside had only needed cosmetic care. Arden chose a booth along the wall and waved to a couple of folks.

Dr. Vet slid into the seat across from her, and she passed him a plastic-coated menu.

He looked around and let out a low whistle. "Did I just stumble onto the set of *Grease?*"

She took a look around as if seeing it through the eyes of a first timer. The checkerboard tile and red vinyl booths screamed time travel. A black and chrome Formica counter stretched across the back with matching red swivel chairs. A jukebox flashed neon in the corner.

She grinned. "I know, right? It hasn't changed since my dad used to bring me here for breakfast when I was a kid." She tipped her chin toward the counter. "We sat over there every time. He'd order eggs and coffee. I had the chocolate chip pancakes with extra whipped cream." Arden noticed his grimace and wondered what she'd said wrong.

He extended his hand. "By the way, I'm Nick Monroe."

Arden sighed in relief. "Oh, thank goodness. It was getting awkward. I couldn't keep thinking of you as Dr. Vet."

"Well, I can't keep thinking of you as Blondie, so..." He quirked an eyebrow.

"Arden Gray. Pleasure meeting you." She'd shaken thousands of hands in her lifetime, but this zap of current was a first.

He freed his hand and rubbed the back of his neck.

Arden wiped hers on her lap. Had he felt it too? Static electricity, probably.

The waitress sauntered over, her cotton candy pink uniform perfectly in theme. Pencil poised, she blew her bangs from her forehead. "Hey, doll. What can I get 'cha?"

Arden smiled. "The usual, Madge, thanks. How's Bert's sciatica?"

"Oh, you know, he likes to complain, so I'm never sure. But he's gettin' 'round easier." After taking their orders, she snapped her gum and strolled away.

Shaking his head, Nick said, "Central casting must have sent her. She's perfect for this place."

Arden grinned. "I doubt they've replaced a saltshaker since the '50s. I half expect the Fonz to bang the jukebox or the Old Man of the Sea to order pie at the counter."

Her chuckle sounded thin, even to her own ears. With her fingers busy rearranging the silverware, she finally cleared her throat. "You must be new in town, or I would have heard about you." As the words passed her lips, she cringed.

He cocked an eyebrow and shot a grin. "So, I'm worthy of the Beacon Bluff gossip mill, am I?"

Arden smoothed the napkin on her lap. "No! I mean, it's off season, and in a town this size nothing goes unnoticed."

"I've only been here a couple of days."

Still fussing with the napkin, she glanced at him. "I, for one, am glad you chose now to visit. I have no idea what I would've done without you."

"I'm happy I could help the little guy." He leaned in. "Next step is to contact animal control."

Her head snapped up so fast she feared she'd need a neck brace. "How can you say such a thing? After what he's been through, that's the last place I'd want him to go. He has feelings, you know."

Nick sat back, hands raised. "Didn't want to assume you were keeping him. You would think I suggested using him as shark bait."

She softened into the booth. "Sorry. I'll take him home when he's ready. In the meantime, I'll post on social media and check with the Coast Guard. Maybe a passing boat has reported losing a dog."

"I doubt we'll find a chip when we scan him. But yeah, I'll alert animal control in case someone comes looking for him. The Coast Guard is a good idea. I wouldn't have thought of that."

Arden shrugged a shoulder. "I know some folks there."

He took a sip of coffee. "We've got to try to find his owner, but my gut tells me he's been abandoned. His condition didn't happen overnight."

Their food arrived. Nick pushed aside his coffee to make room for his egg white and spinach omelet. He grimaced as Arden smeared butter on her French toast, then flooded her plate with syrup.

She frowned. Her late husband had judged her food choices too. She refused to be sugar shamed.

Mentally shrugging, she moved on. "Hurricane Camilla blew through here two years ago. Totally devastated the town. Many evacuees never came back for their pets. He may be one of the last casualties."

Nick tilted his head in thought. "That would make sense, given his condition. He's malnourished and weak."

She set down her fork and met his gaze. "He'll be fine. You get him healthy, and I'll take it from there."

Before Nick could respond, her brother Colin approached, glancing at her. Then he slapped Nick on the back. "There you are. I thought we had a meeting this morning."

"Sorry, dude. I went for an early run and got sidetracked." Nick sipped his coffee and nodded at Arden.

Colin turned to her, clearly confused. "Hey, sis. I didn't think you knew Nick from my college days. He's staying at the house."

Wrinkling her nose, she said, "Actually, I didn't."

Nick spoke up. "I saved her dog from drowning."

Colin's eyes narrowed. "Wait a minute. She doesn't own a dog."

"She does now. Long story." Nick's gaze bounced between the siblings.

They'd been mistaken for twins as kids with just eighteen months between them and the same sandy blond hair, though hers had curls—the bane of her existence—while Colin's was wavy. And the same blue-green eyes—though Colin's reminded her of a churning sea while hers were...well, green. Still, the resemblance was there.

"That's why you looked familiar," Nick said. "Now I vaguely remember the family pictures he had in our room. Different last name threw me off."

Yeah, well, marriage changed more than a last name.

Colin pushed into the booth without asking. After signaling Madge for a cup of coffee, he turned to Arden, "You look awful."

"Gee, thanks. Love you too." Arden didn't need a mirror or her brother to remind her of what she already knew. Scrubs the color of nausea medication, as well as the swollen aftermath of a crying jag, weren't doing her any favors.

Colin grinned. "Just keeping it real."

He accepted a mug from Madge, then turned to Nick. "I'm looking forward to finalizing the Vets Without Boundaries numbers. Dad's excited to welcome you into the ministry network as soon as our board approves your final budget."

Nick chewed so aggressively on a bite of melon, Arden feared for his molars. He kept his eyes focused on the Formica tabletop, clearly uncomfortable with this topic. "I'm finalizing the numbers now."

Arden took a swig of Diet Coke. "What's this all about?"

"Nick's partnering with H3 to start a veterinarian ministry.

He's staying with me at the house while we verify the projected numbers before he joins Mom and Dad in Honduras."

Just when she had begun to warm to the man—platonically, of course. But now, learning of his connection with her parents' ministry, friendship was a long shot. While proud of her parents' work, she couldn't forget what their ministry had cost her.

The Bennetts had begun Honduras Has Hope, dubbed H3 for simplicity, after their early retirement. The Charlotte church they had started as newlyweds had grown into one of the first nationally recognized mega-churches. After stepping down, they had moved to Honduras, building H3 into a multi-faceted relief organization near San Pedro Sula. Now they lived in Honduras full time while Colin ran the stateside operation out of his home in Beacon Bluff.

She licked syrup from her fingertips. "Veterinarian ministry? No offense, but I don't think the villages H3 serves worry about family pets when their kids need food."

Colin gave her a look. "You do realize that saying 'no offense' doesn't make it less offensive."

She shrugged. "It's a valid observation. Every summer after we stopped coming to Beacon Bluff, I saw what those families went through. I may not be part of the ministry now, but I still care about the poverty those families live with."

Nick pushed his plate away. "It's okay. I get that reaction a lot." He turned his focus toward her. "There's more to veterinary science than puppies and kittens. Diseased livestock can wreck economies. Rabies can devastate communities."

She dropped her gaze. "Point taken."

"Like I said, it's not the first time I've had to defend my ministry."

"Well, I didn't have to be rude. Thanks for being gracious."

A strained silence pressed down on them.

Seemingly oblivious, Colin continued to drink his coffee and sat back. "Assuming the numbers pan out, you'll be heading to Honduras soon."

Her brother's statement put the nail in the coffin of any hope for friendship between herself and Nick. She would not sacrifice anything else to Honduras—even if he was just a friend.

Madge dropped the check, and Arden snatched it before she shoved her brother from the booth.

"We really need to get going." She glanced over her shoulder. "Ready to head back to the beach?" She didn't wait for a reply.

Nick told Colin he'd see him back at his house and caught up to her at the register. "Hey, this was going to be my treat."

Without looking at him, she tapped her card to the reader. "No need. It's not like this was a date."

Oh no, had she said that out loud? Arden closed her eyes. *A date, Arden? Seriously?*

She dropped her card before she could stuff it back into her pocket, refusing to look his way. "I'm happy to pay for that ridiculously healthy breakfast as a thank you for saving my dog."

He chuckled. "Okay. I'll buy next time. You can order as much processed sugar as you want."

She looked over her shoulder on her way out. "What makes you think there'll be a next time?"

NICK SHOOK HIS HEAD. He had to admire Arden's no-next-time exit line. Unfortunately, she ruined its impact by running smack dab into Tiffany Meyers. Literally.

The scene unfolded like a Three Stooges bit, complete with a dramatic *oomph*. Both women stumbled backward, and Arden clutched the reporter's arms for balance, which only made things wobblier. They flailed in tandem until Tiffany righted herself by grabbing a nearby lamp post.

As for Arden? She wasn't as fortunate. She tripped over the daddy-long-leg scrub pants and sailed out of her clown-size crocs like a cartoon character.

Nick lunged, hoping to save her from a face plant and his arm circled her midsection, pulling her against his chest—where a chuckle was trying to stage a jailbreak.

He cleared his throat. "Everyone okay here?" His grin was so wide, it was a wonder his lips didn't touch his earlobes.

Both women stiffened like they'd been flash-frozen, and Tiffany's glare could have incinerated concrete.

Wisely, he swallowed the snicker about to bust loose.

Arden, breathless and mortified, managed, "I'm so sorry, Ms. Meyers. You're not hurt, are you?"

Tiffany shook her head, blinking back surprise like a news anchor caught without hairspray. "Not at all. I was hoping to find you and Dr. Monroe. I didn't make the best impression at the clinic this morning and wanted to apologize." Her words were friendly, but her expression suggested a hidden agenda. Her gaze lingered on Nick's arm, still bracketed around Arden.

As if registering their compromising position, Arden stepped sideways. "Ms. Meyers—"

"Tiffany, please. I hope you won't hold my first impression against me. I may work in cable news, but my real passion is animal welfare. I foster, I volunteer—basically I run a one-woman rescue service out of my apartment." She arched a brow, turning an awkward moment into a shared laugh.

Nick chuckled and nodded. "As a vet, I can't fault your enthusiasm. Did you make an appointment with Stella?"

"I was actually hoping to speak to you both. I'd love to feature the dog's rescue on our network. What do you think? Can we set something up?"

Arden's smile iced over, making Nick think she was about to audition for the lead role in *Frozen*. "I'm afraid I'm not available."

Nick tilted his head, eyebrows lifting in a playful dare. "Why not hear her out? Could be fun."

"Fun is funnel cake and Ferris wheels, not talking in front of a camera. I'm sorry, but we need to get back to the beach." Arden tightened her lips and spun on her heel with all the grace of a retreating queen.

Tiffany reached out, resting a hand on Arden's arm. "This would be such a feel-good piece. What can I say to change your mind?"

Arden looked toward the sky, heaved a sigh, then turned back. "I realize it's off season, but is the news cycle this desperate?"

Tiffany shrugged. "Well, there is that. Hurricane Camilla did a number on our pet population. One happy ending might inspire others to adopt another abandoned animal"

Nick mentally gave her bonus points. Manipulative? Sure. Effective? Probably.

"I'm sure Dr. Monroe could handle the interview without me."

"There's more than one hero here. You rushed into the surf and Dr. Monroe came along for the rescue. I'm afraid it's the three of you or none of you."

"Then none of us it is." Arden crossed her arms like an iron gate.

Nick saw his future circle the drain. She had no idea she was jeopardizing future support for his ministry.

Tiffany winked. "Arden, talk it over with Nick—maybe over a candlelit dinner? Men can be shockingly persuasive over a basket of breadsticks."

"Dr. Monroe is not—"

Nick jumped in. "Honey, there's no harm in talking it over." He threw the reporter a quick glance. "That work for you?"

Tiffany nodded, eyes gleaming. "Knew it. A rescue, a budding romance—social media will eat you up."

Judging by Arden's deepening frown and laser-beam glare,

Nick guessed social media fans would be eating roadkill. He knew he had crossed a line by interrupting her and calling her honey.

If five-foot-five blonde fury could self-combust, Nick would be following a pillar of fire across the street.

# CHAPTER 3

*A*rden beat Nick to the car and he cringed noting how she sat fuming behind the steering wheel—eyes locked ahead, jaw clenched tight enough to crack enamel. Getting through to her wasn't going to be easy.

He tapped on the window. "I'll be right back. Going to check on our patient." A brief break from each other might lower the car's interior temperature a few degrees.

Relieved the dog remained stable, Nick returned quickly. "Recovery's going well. He's quite a handsome fellow now that Stella has cleaned him up. No microchip though. He's sleeping, which is the best thing for him."

Arden's shoulders eased, her sigh of relief audible. Even a fleeting smile. "I'm so glad. Let's hope he has sweet dreams."

Nick let the silence settle as she pulled into traffic. Not a comfortable silence, exactly, but progress. He hadn't meant to set her off. In hindsight, piggybacking on the reporter's assumption hadn't been his finest moment. Still, with his ministry funding on life support, this interview could attract donations. Just a thought, but not one he could afford to ignore.

He cleared his throat. "Should we talk about the interview? I'd appreciate you considering it."

"What possessed you to tell a reporter that we are a couple? We've known each other for three hours." Her voice escalated to full-caps mode. She kept her focus straight ahead. "We are not a couple!"

"Okay, not my best decision. But is it such a bad idea? It bought us some time to talk before flat-out refusing."

"She's a reporter. Discretion isn't their strong suit. I don't need this complication in my life. I've got enough on my plate—especially now that I have a dog depending on me."

"How long can a television interview take? One interview isn't a large time commitment."

"You don't know what I've got going on. But you know who does? Me! We can discuss this until the cows come home and I won't be changing my mind." She turned on the radio, upping the volume.

He could take a hint.

Arden turned into the drive and eased up the rise toward her home. Earlier, in the chaos, Nick hadn't noticed the location. He let out a low whistle. "You live in a lighthouse?"

She glanced over, tension slipping into a soft smile.

"Yes. I sure do."

Before them stood a two-story red brick house with black shutters and a wide wrap-around porch with a white-posted railing skirting three sides. But the main event was the looming cylinder behind the residence.

The lighthouse seemed to poke the clouds. It was, by design, the most commanding presence on the shoreline. Constructed from brick, but painted white for nighttime visibility, its ebony dome capped a beacon, circled by a narrow outdoor iron gallery. Right beneath the gallery, where it met the brick, were tall red diamonds.

The click of a seatbelt pulled his attention back to Arden.

"Thanks again for this morning. Please invoice me for the cost of treatment." She climbed out of the SUV hugging her arms.

There was a breeze blowing off the ocean, so maybe she was trying to conserve warmth. But Nick sensed vulnerability.

He followed, hands on his hips, eyes on the tower. "Oh no, you don't. You can't just drop a lighthouse and walk away."

The wind swept her hair from her eyes as she looked up. "When I was a kid—before my parents focused on Honduras—we spent our summers here. This lighthouse was everything. I'd draw pictures of it, do research projects about it, and counted down the days until our next visit." Her face lost a bit of its light. "Then we began spending summers in Honduras."

She turned back toward him.

"We used to rent Colin's place. I remember staring out of my window, the lighthouse beam lulling me to sleep."

Nick settled against her SUV. He enjoyed this nostalgic version of Arden. "How'd you end up owning it? Did someone just throw a for sale sign out front?"

She chuckled. "The United States Coast Guard sometimes decommissions lighthouses. This one went to a historical foundation—until the CEO got busted siphoning funds to bankroll his secret, second family. I saw the sale notice in *The Charlotte Observer*, and here we are now."

"My heart goes out to both of the CEO's families, but his fall from grace was definitely your gain." He hesitated. "So, it's just you living here?"

She didn't quite meet his eyes. "Yes."

Nick glanced at his watch and straightened. "I need to check in with the clinic and circle back to Colin." He back peddled down the hill toward the beach. "Stop by the clinic and we'll plan what's next for your little guy." With that, he turned and broke into a steady stride heading back to where he left his truck.

Nick reached his Dodge pickup, thankful it ran better than it looked. Quite the contrast to Arden's sleek luxury SUV. But what Ole Red lacked in style, it more than made up for with reliability.

Leaning on the side of the door, Nick stretched and considered the morning's events. Saving animals got his heart pumping. That's why he'd become a vet in the first place. People cared about their pets, and treating one often opened the door to sharing God's love.

That little dog mattered to Arden. He saw it in her desperation, the way she clung to hope. The dog might not have been hers when she found him, but he was now.

And Arden. Well, she wasn't just strikingly beautiful. She radiated something—compassion, fire, stubborn resilience. What would that hair look like when she wore it down? And those eyes... They reflected a kaleidoscope of thought—distress, humor, and snapping annoyance. Each emotion brought out its own shade of blue-green.

Despite the tears that had been involved, Nick smiled as he recalled her breakdown at the clinic. He had to give her credit, she hadn't let her emotions loose until after the emergency had passed.

And what was up with that handshake at the diner? It seemed as if the sizzle had been mutual.

Sure, she was gorgeous. But there was something more drawing him in, like a white cat to dark clothes. There was a blend of feisty vulnerability, competence, and insecurity. Somewhere inside, he sensed there was a confident woman trying to claw her way out.

It had been a while since anyone had caught his eye. Perhaps it was simply that he was overdue in the romance department.

But he had no intention of exploring this nonsense. He had a God-given mission to launch and had no time for a relationship. Not even with a woman who sent tingles tripping up his arm from a mere handshake.

Once before, a woman had distracted him from his ministry,

and it could have been a disaster. It was best to avoid the whole mess. No matter how much he might like to get to know Arden Gray better, he wouldn't—no, couldn't—indulge himself.

He settled into the driver's seat, resting his head against the cracked vinyl. Romance was the least of his worries. He'd spent the night hacking away at the Vets Without Boundaries budget. In desperation, he'd even changed the calculator batteries. No miracle there.

Nick had eliminated his wants and had cut his needs to the bone. The only line items left would cut out the soul of the ministry. Anymore and it wouldn't survive.

Colin's family had been generous, but their support had limits. He wasn't the only one in need of their resources. What if they deemed Vets Without Boundaries no longer worth the investment?

His morning run had been more prayer than cardio. He knew God had called him to serve in Honduras. Every locked door had opened, affirming Nick's belief.

If this failed...it would be on him.

His phone buzzed with a text, pulling him from his introspection. A grin spread across his face and he laughed out loud. The text congratulated him on becoming a finalist for a Faith Works Foundation grant. *I hear you, Lord.*

The Faith Works grant was a coveted prize in the world of faith-based nonprofits, with countless worthy ministries applying each year. The last statistic he'd seen showed that fewer than ten percent made it to the finalist stage.

The winner would be announced at the Faith Works Gala in a couple of months. And, as luck would have it, this year's event was being held right here in Beacon Bluff, hosted by Honduras Has Hope.

Nick didn't believe in coincidences. The fact that this text came through while he was actively petitioning God only strengthened his resolve. He would do whatever it took to position Vets Without Boundaries for success.

Now more than ever, he had no time for extracurricular distractions. Even the ones with wild blonde hair, a lighthouse, and a rescued dachshund.

He fired up the engine and put the truck in gear. Time to get to work.

∼

ARDEN STEPPED out of the first-floor primary bath. The building's original purpose had been as an officer's quarters for the Atlantic Region of the U. S. Coast Guard.

The foundation's CEO had spared no expense renovating the downstairs. Unfortunately, pesky indictments and frozen assets had prevented any work upstairs. That's where she came in.

While showering, she had recapped the morning's events. Walking on the beach after a sleepless night. Rushing into the ocean to rescue a drowning dog. Encountering a man too good looking for his own good. Embarrassing herself in front of said man.

Of course, it wasn't a date. Of all the ridiculous things to pop out of her mouth. The shower spray rinsed tension from her muscles, but Arden's mind hadn't relaxed one bit.

The first good looking man she'd interacted with on a personal level since her husband's death and she abandoned rational thought...as if she had been the one battered by the ocean and spit out on shore. At least she'd have had the excuse of a potential head injury.

The state of her sanity notwithstanding, Arden resolved to refuse any television interviews. Her late husband, ever eager to use her for his own gain, had pushed her into the spotlight, and it had been a disaster. She had no desire to re-live that nightmare, no matter how noble the cause.

Her thoughts melted whenever she thought of the dog who had been thrust into her arms by the relentless surf. Painfully prominent ribs, tangled coat. Eyes sunken and pleading.

Despite the warm shower, she shuddered to think of the unyielding power of the ocean currents and the poor pup ineffectively struggling against the tide.

Arden knew how awful it felt to be trapped. Oh, not physically like the pup, but her situation had left her feeling almost as helpless. She had been bound by her own inadequacies and the perceived inability to improve her life. But no more. She had plans to reclaim her strength.

Swaddled in towels—one around her body, the other perched like a crown on her head—Arden strutted down the hallway on a noble quest for Diet Coke. She stopped cold.

There was noise coming from the kitchen.

Cabinet doors opening. Closing. Rustling.

Someone was *in* there.

Perfect. Because nothing says "good morning" like a drowning dog and a home invasion.

Okay, okay...think.

She was wrapped in nothing but a towel and her phone was in the kitchen with the intruder. She had all the combat readiness of a baby chick.

She needed a weapon.

She needed...an umbrella.

She grabbed it off the hook, flattened herself against the wall, and channeled every cop show she'd ever binge-watched.

One steadying breath. Umbrella raised. Showtime.

She stormed into the kitchen like a caffeinated ninja.

A man in a hoodie turned from the fridge just in time to catch a whack to the head.

"Ow! What the—"

"Colin?" Her towel nearly slipped. "You scared ten years off my life!"

He groaned, rubbing the back of his head. "Why did you hit me?"

"You broke into my house!"

"You gave me a key!" He nodded toward the spare lying on the counter.

"That was for emergencies," she shouted.

"Your car was out front, so I knew you were home. When you didn't answer, I figured you were getting dressed or something. I thought—hey, no big deal, I'll just grab a snack while I wait." Colin turned his attention back to the refrigerator. "Ah, here we go." He took out the apple pie, cut himself a generous slice, and stuck it in the microwave.

After the beep, he grabbed a fork and turned back to Arden, groaning at the first taste. "Your baking is out of this world." Colin continued around his second bite, "What's this about you owning a dog?"

"I found him on the beach while I was walking this morning. He's the sweetest thing. Too bad he's still at the vet clinic. I could have used a watch dog," she said, giving her brother a scathing glare.

An unrepentant grin found its way around his mouthful of pie, and Arden shook her head. She never had been able to resist him.

Arden ducked into the laundry room off the kitchen and found jeans and a lightweight baby blue sweater. Calling out to her brother while she dressed, she filled him in on the details of the rescue. She walked back into the kitchen, finger drying her hair as she pulled a stool up to the granite-topped island. "I've got to say, your friend Nick certainly saved the day."

After a beat of silence, Colin leveled a solemn look her way as he took another bite of pie. "So, how are you doing?"

"Other than having years shaved off my life...thanks to you? Fine."

"You can't distract me by picking a fight."

She groaned and pushed damp hair off her face. "It's the one-year anniversary of Lincoln's death, okay? Happy now?"

"Hardly. But maybe you need to talk about it."

"What is there to talk about? I'm fine."

"Your future, for starters. You've been in Beacon Bluff a month now. I understand you needed time to regroup. But, Den, it's been a year. Don't you think it's time for you to join H3?"

Despite his use of the nickname only he was allowed to use, Arden pressed her fingers on the pressure point between her eyes. "Colin, how many times have I told you? I will not be joining H3. Not now. Not ever."

His gaze softened and his stance relaxed. "Arden, come home. Let us take care of you. Mom and Dad are worried."

Of all the words in the English language that he could have strung together, he chose the worst. Now they were worried? After abandoning her before her final year of high school?

Arden struggled to not raise her voice. "Come home? That's the last thing I plan to do."

It was no wonder she fell so fast for Lincoln's promises of love and security. Craving the love and support, she had expected her husband to take care of her. What had she been thinking? He'd turned out to be as reliable as a foundation built on sinking sand.

She shoved away the memories of that time in her life. She had no intention of looking over her shoulder. These days, she focused on the brighter horizon.

Colin set his plate in the sink. "When are you going to forgive them for moving to Honduras?"

"Is that what you think this is all about? Some effort to get back at our parents?"

He rubbed his hands across his face. "I'm handling this poorly. The family is concerned for you. We love you and want to see you happy. But also, you have a lot to offer the ministry and we could really use you."

"I love H3 and I'm proud of what you, Mom, and Dad are

building in Honduras. You're exactly where God wants you." She shrugged. "But it's not where I belong."

"Are you sure? Have you even considered it?"

She couldn't believe he was asking. "Of course I have. I love the country and its people. But God isn't nudging me in that direction." She had spent much of the past year on her knees, petitioning divine guidance. Honduras had never felt right.

"Where is He nudging?"

As she looked at Colin , she took several moments to consider their shared history. Growing up, Colin had always been her closest friend and confidant, especially because they were pastor's kids, which tended to create distance from others their age. Just under two years older than she, he'd remained the same dependable presence—except for that time when he ran away from the restrictions and expectations that came with being John and Lila Bennett's son.

Nonetheless, Arden had kept her plans close to her vest, not ready to expose them to the family's well-intentioned, yet critical scrutiny. On the off chance they liked the idea, she feared their enthusiasm would take over and, yet again, Arden would be relegated to a supporting role.

But she respected Colin's business sense. H3 had thrived under his watch. And, unlike her parents, if he pushed, she could push back.

Taking a deep breath, she stepped out on faith. "I'm turning the lighthouse into a bed and breakfast."

Colin narrowed his eyes as she watched his brain whir. "Not a bad idea. But Beacon Bluff's tourism industry hasn't rebounded from Hurricane Camilla. Where are your guests going to come from?"

Leave it to Colin to pinpoint her biggest fear. "I'm working on that."

"What's your marketing plan?"

"Working on it. I've been meeting with the Charlotte lawyers to set up a non-profit organization. Part of my plan is to have the first level of the lighthouse become a museum to attract visitors."

Colin leaned back on the counter and crossed his arms. "You know nothing about setting up or running a museum."

Arden scorched him with a look. "I've negotiated with one of the regional museum boards to set it up and keep it running. I'm donating the space and all the historical items I've found in the attic."

Colin nodded in approval. "Good thinking. So, where are you getting your guests from again?"

"The usual places. Ads in regional magazines, social media, word of mouth."

"Seems a bit passive, if you ask me."

"I didn't. I said I'm still working on it."

"I guess if you don't figure it out, we're back to you joining H3." Colin shrugged as if it were no big deal.

As if this weren't her life they were talking about. As if he had no faith in her ability to succeed on her own. No husband. No family. Just her.

In the twelve months since her husband's death, she had been alone. Oh, she had friends in Charlotte, but they were couple friends. They hadn't known what to do with her once she was widowed—especially under the circumstances. Honestly, she was friends with them only because Lincoln hand-picked them.

Since his passing, she'd had plenty of time to reflect on her life. One conclusion rang loud and clear—it was time to take control, not just react to whatever came her way.

Her parents left her, she hadn't complained.

It was clear her family wanted her to marry Lincoln, so she did.

Well, not anymore. She wasn't going to allow Colin to perpetuate that pattern or tempt her to fall back into the old habit of letting others define her future.

Anger burned in her chest, but her words caught on a swell of hurt. "Just...go," she said, her voice breaking. "I thought—if nothing else—I could count on you."

Colin held her tight, even as she resisted. "You know I love you. I believe in you. I know you're capable. That's exactly why I want you to join H3. But sometimes, being smart and capable just isn't enough."

"No, but God is. I firmly believe he wants me in Beacon Bluff."

Colin let her go and looked to the side. "I won't argue with your faith. But speaking from experience, it's easy to mistake our own desires for God's will." He turned back to her, softer now. "I'm just glad you've got H3 as a backup...in case it comes to that."

Arden set her jaw. "I know you're thick-headed, so let me try again. I'll not be moving to Honduras."

"Time will tell. It might not seem like it, but I do hope your bed and breakfast is a success." He rubbed his hand over the back of his head. "And as for being thick-headed, it's a good thing. Protects me from umbrella attacks." Colin brushed past her on his way to the door, giving her still-damp hair a playful tug. "Now that I've got my sister back, I actually want to spend time with her."

Arden swallowed hard. Her marriage had cost her a lot, but nothing more so than the closeness she had once shared with her brother.

Colin and Lincoln had circled each other like predators, always testing boundaries, always asserting control—especially over her.

"I don't need to join the family business for us to spend time together."

"Especially since I have a key." He held it up and tucked it into his pocket. "Thanks for the pie."

"You're lucky it was only an umbrella."

# CHAPTER 4

$\mathcal{N}$ick handed Stella a chart and watched as Arden walked into the clinic. The soundtrack of his professional life would assault her ears, he was sure. A symphony of barks and yips greeted her as she sidestepped a lunging chihuahua.

He chuckled as she approached the front desk. "I see you've met Goliath. Come on back."

Arden grinned. "The name suits him."

They entered a large room with one wall of closed doors that opened into treatment rooms. From a layman's perspective, would she see clutter or the organized chaos that saved lives and protected pets? Counters lined the other three walls with clear-front cabinets overhead. A sink, a few computer monitors, various pieces of lab equipment, and a countertop refrigerator took center stage. Two stainless steel exam tables stood in the middle. This space, full of veterinary paraphernalia, was as comfortable to him as his favorite Nikes.

Their star patient sat in the crate of honor on one table, kept close by the comings and goings of vet staff for careful monitoring.

Arden claimed a rolling stool and slid over to the dog.

He lifted his head and thumped his tail.

Her smile could have powered the whole building. "Look how handsome you are."

*Calm down. She's referring to the dog, you idiot.*

The dog no longer smelled like dead fish, but his hip bones still jutted from his lackluster fur. He looked more like a rusted penny instead of a freshly minted one.

Nick could count his vertebrae without an X-ray and feared the weight of his head would tip him nose-first. Even his tail was scrawny.

Arden didn't seem to notice. She cooed over how dapper he looked, how bright his eyes were. She scratched him under the chin, describing all the fun they would have together.

The dog licked her hand and tried to wiggle his hind end. He was clearly smitten.

Nick walked toward the crate. "Want me to take him out so you can hold him?"

The wattage of her smile made his eyes widen.

He gently handed the pup over and she rocked him like a baby against her chest.

Nick leaned a hip against the counter. "Did you touch base with the Coast Guard?"

"I stopped by earlier. No reports of lost dogs. No hits from social media either. While I'm sad no one misses him, I would have struggled to give him up." She snuggled him and earned a snuffle against her ear.

"Have you thought of a name?"

Arden tilted her head and regarded him closely. "I could call him Red for his fur." She wrinkled her nose. "Sweet Pea isn't bad, but he's much too distinguished for that." She cuddled the dog's head beneath her chin. "Do you have any thoughts?"

"Maybe something nautical. Jack—as in Sparrow? Nemo?"

"Hmm..." She narrowed her eyes, then grinned. "I know. Jonah. They both washed up on shore."

"Yeah, well. Let's hope he's more obedient than his namesake."

Holding the dog away from her chest, she declared, "I officially christen you Jonah Gray." Instead of a sword to the shoulder, she knighted him by kissing his head.

Satisfied, he snuggled back into her arms.

Nick couldn't help watching her every move. It surely made her uncomfortable given her flushed cheeks. Despite her discomfort, he couldn't look away. Her blend of strength and vulnerability intrigued him—a puzzle his brain refused to ignore.

"Maybe we can catch dinner sometime."

*Smooth. What was he? A middle-schooler?*

If he could yank those impulsive words back, he'd swallow them whole. He knew better than to let his mouth get ahead of his brain.

Arden blinked so fast she reminded him of windshield wipers.

Accustomed to skittish animals, he recognized the panic. He hadn't thought it possible for her to focus more on the dog than she was. But she managed.

"Uh...well, I...um..." After an excruciating beat, she exhaled. "Thanks for asking, but no."

Nick frowned. "That's it? No?"

"No, thank you."

He should feel relieved. He shouldn't feel so...put out. His frown stayed in place. "Because I'm your brother's friend?"

She shook her head, far more interested in Jonah than with the idea of having dinner with him.

While Nick wasn't a ladies' man, he did okay. "Maybe it's because I'm your dog's doctor?" Even he knew that sounded ridiculous, but at least it got a laugh.

"Nick, you're a great guy..."

"Isn't it early for the 'it's not you, it's me' speech?"

"Not if it's the truth." She scratched Jonah's ear. "I'm recently widowed. I'm not interested in dating."

"You were married?"

"My husband died in a car accident."

Nick hung his head. Great. He was hitting on a widow. He'd missed the significance of her and Colin's last names being different. One more reason to shut this down before it grew roots.

He looked up. "Arden, I had no idea. If I had, I wouldn't have asked. May I ask how long you've been alone?"

She paused. "Lincoln's been gone a year."

"I truly am sorry. For your loss. And my insensitivity."

She shrugged and gently returned Jonah to his crate. "When can he come home?"

Right. Back to business. Her dog was his patient, and her brother was his best friend. That had to be the line he wouldn't cross.

She sat back down as Nick turned to the computer and reviewed the dog's recent vitals and progress notes. "As long as his blood oxygen levels continue to improve and his lungs are clear, he should be able to go home in a day or so. We'll give you detailed instructions on his at-home care, and you'll need to bring him in for follow-ups."

Her lack of response stretched the silence, amplifying the yips and yaps coming from the waiting room.

Nick shifted his weight, hyperaware of each tick from the clock and the low hum of the fluorescent bulbs. He racked his brain for something to say. "Have you given any more thought to the television interview?"

Arden's eyes narrowed and she shook her head, but still, she said nothing.

"Jonah is doing well. He'll be camera ready in no time."

Her jaw tensed and it seemed as if she was grinding her teeth.

His effort to lighten the mood was an epic failure.

"Why would you say that? I've already refused to participate in any interview."

Frustration surged from his stomach to the back of his throat. It was one thing to turn him down socially, especially given her past, but why was she being so stubborn on this? A few minutes talking about a dog. How hard could it be?

This interview could be the break he needed to impress the Faith Works' selection committee. What did they say? Any publicity is good publicity? Saving a dog would be great publicity. He couldn't pass up this golden opportunity.

Nick didn't exactly yell, but he didn't try to hide his resentment either. She didn't seem to be taking the matter as seriously as he would like. "Why are you being so unreasonable?"

She stood quickly, the wheeled stool knocking into a nearby cabinet. Arden advanced, pointing her finger at him. "You have no say in what I do. You don't need to understand it, you don't need to agree, but you do need to respect my decision."

He had wondered if her modern-day Valkyrie only came out with pushy reporters.

But here she was now, in full living color.

He pushed his hands through his hair and groaned. He closed his eyes and took a series of calming breaths. She wasn't wrong. But time was running out and hopelessness was knocking at his door.

Tense moments passed before he felt her hand on his forearm. "Nick, why is this interview so important to you?"

Nick was tempted to confide in her. Share with her his fear of failing. All about the pit that yawned in his stomach each time he reviewed the budget.

But she was Colin's sister, a part of the family who would determine the future of Vets Without Boundaries. Her loyalty would surely be with them. He couldn't take the chance of confiding his fears and then having her share them with her brother. He needed to be the one to break the news to Colin and John Bennett.

Instead, he decided to give her less information. "As someone who grew up in ministry, you know this life revolves around finding financial support. I can't justify turning publicity away from Vets Without Boundaries. And honestly, your refusal to cooperate baffles me. Tiffany made it clear she wouldn't go forward without your participation. What are you afraid of?"

He was fascinated, watching the stubbornness creep back into her body. Shoulders straightened, jaw tightened, lips pressed into a thin line.

Hands on her hips, she met his gaze with a defiant tilt of her chin. "I'm not afraid." She gave Jonah a quick kiss and stormed out the door.

Nick caught the shadow of pain pass through her eyes. Oh, the fear was there. Maybe it ran so deep she hadn't dared drag it into the light—maybe she never would. But one thing was certain. Even after their disagreement, the room felt dimmer the moment she was gone.

ARDEN RUSHED FROM THE CLINIC, thankful Stella was too busy to chat. She drew a deep breath and set a brisk pace to anywhere. Only the end of the pier stopped her from taking a header into the ocean.

She took down her hair and let it blow free, her face turned into the wind.

Why would Nick ask her to dinner? He hadn't taken her careless comment at the diner seriously, had he? Did he think she was angling for a date? Well, if that were the case, she'd surely set him straight by turning him down.

Maybe it was her vibe—something that inadvertently signaled she was in the market for a man. *Hope not.*

Because she wasn't shopping for another heartache.

But why, then, had she allowed Nick to believe she mourned a dead husband when the truth was that she grieved the loss of a happily-ever-after? If she were honest with herself, she would admit it was a way to put distance between them.

Just being near him was enough to leave her breathless. He made her want to run away, not from fear, but from self-preservation. He made her feel things that her current life and goals simply didn't allow for.

Still, the temptation to say yes to the date had almost overwhelmed her. Reluctantly, she acknowledged she was lonely. An evening out, exchanging laughs across a table with Nick...it sounded too good to be true. And, as everyone knew, if it sounded too good to be true, it probably was.

Her late husband's words showed up uninvited.

*"You need to stay up-to-date on current events, Arden. You had nothing interesting to contribute during dinner with the Parnells."*

Then...

*"You're such a quiet thing. Where's your personality, Arden?"*

Arden ran her hands through her hair trying to rub away those words—and others like them. She hadn't fit in with Lincoln's associates and their wives, no getting around it. What made her think she'd be an interesting dinner date for a man like Nick? Kind. Accomplished. Confident.

Time spent with Nick would cost more than she could afford. Even if he was the one picking up the dinner tab.

The most important lesson learned from her marriage was that a relationship could not make her happy. She had a Ph.D. in regret. Arden refused to make that error in judgment again. With God's grace, she would choreograph her own happily ever after.

And then there was this reporter debacle. How dare Nick try to run roughshod over her decision not to do the interview. Just like a man. Just like her family. Assuming she would submit to their greater wisdom. Well, not this time. Never again would she cave for someone else's agenda.

A small gremlin voice wormed its way into her thoughts. Could Nick be right about the fear factor? Could she be hiding behind her past failures, allowing Lincoln to win yet again?

She groaned, bending to rest her forehead against her hands while holding onto the railing. What Nick said about publicity gave her pause. Non-profits weren't the only enterprise television exposure could benefit.

Colin's interrogation regarding where she'd find guests for Keeper's Quarters taunted her. She needed to think like a businesswoman, not a downtrodden wife.

If she wanted to step into a new future, she had to turn her back on old insecurities.

Her stomach fluttered, an anxious twist cycling tight. She could do this. Which meant her new priority was clear—keeping her distance from Nick Monroe. Which shouldn't be too difficult since he had a one-way ticket to Honduras in his back pocket.

Arden walked back to the clinic where she had left her car, her thoughts racing. Instead of worrying about a nonexistent date with Nick Monroe, she needed to throw herself body and soul into creating a five-star bed and breakfast.

Even if it meant stepping back in front of a camera.

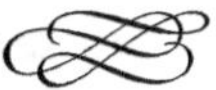

# CHAPTER 5

*N*ick jogged along the beach, his rhythmic strides leaving marks in the sand. No signs of a dog—or damsel—in distress. Not that he was looking.

Who was he trying to kid? It was no coincidence that ever since they rescued Jonah, he had run this same stretch of beach at the exact same time hoping to run into Arden.

He felt uneasy about how things ended between them at the clinic. He knew he shouldn't have pushed her about doing the interview, but her lack of cooperation had irritated him. In the heat of the moment, he'd let his frustration get the best of him and ended up accusing her of being a coward for not agreeing to the interview. What a jerk move. He realized he had no right to assume her motives for refusal.

He needed to clear the air.

Nick had earned a reputation for being easy-going, and that was by design. His father's role as an interim pastor meant their family frequently moved from one small church to another, making it challenging to form lasting connections. To cope with this constant change, Nick made a conscious decision early on to be friendly and sociable with everyone, never diving deep with anyone. This approach allowed him to blend in while still managing to avoid emotional attachments.

As he approached the lighthouse, the familiar wooden stairs came into view. There she was, sitting on the bottom step, gazing out over the ocean.

The wind tangled her hair and, as she brushed it away from her face, she noticed him. Sending him a smile, it seemed soft yet tinged with uncertainty, as if she was unsure of her reception.

She needn't have worried.

Nick grinned and sat beside her. "Find any lost dogs lately?"

He was rewarded with her husky chuckle. "I think one's enough, don't you? I wouldn't wish that experience on any other animal."

They both turned their faces back toward the water's edge, watching seagulls dip and dive. Glimmering patches of sunlight broke through the clouds and the air was thick with the smell of salt, seaweed, and damp sand. The sun was about to complete its ascent into the sky, leaving golden orange streaks behind.

Without glancing his way, she said, "Against my better judgment, I've decided to agree to the interview."

Nick wasn't sure he'd heard correctly. The wind could have messed with her words. Did she just say she'd do the interview?

He rubbed his face with both hands, taken aback by the intensity of his relief. It hit him like a wave, overwhelming and unexpected. Yes, he had hoped for it, but he never dared believe it would happen. "Arden, thank you. This exposure could be what turns Vets Without Boundaries into a reality."

She fixed her gaze on his face, looking puzzled. Leaning forward, she rested an elbow on her knee and propped her chin in her hand. "I don't get it. Colin said things are looking good on H3's end. Isn't that enough? Why does this interview even matter?"

He looked down, kicking the loose sand beneath his feet,

readying himself to share his concerns. "The numbers your brother and dad want to confirm? Well, they don't match the original proposal. By a lot." Nick glanced at his hands resting on his thighs. "I'd appreciate it if you didn't share this information with your family. I will talk this over with them on our next conference call."

Arden nodded and waved her hand. "That's fine. It's not my story to tell, and I have nothing to do with H3. But you're still not making any sense. It's not like Tiffany will pay us for the interview," she pointed out, her confusion evident.

"No, but she can put my ministry in front of potential supporters. The cable news channel has a wide reach throughout the southeast, so it's an excellent opportunity for exposure. Besides, I just learned that Vets Without Boundaries is a finalist for a Faith Works grant, and the selection committee likes to see investment in the local community."

"That's great news about Faith Works. That's no easy achievement. They're very selective."

The approval shining from her eyes meant more to him than it should. "That's why this interview is so important," he admitted, his voice tinged with an unexpected vulnerability.

A vee formed between her brows. "Don't you think H3 would cover the difference?"

He shrugged. "I'm not naïve enough to believe H3 doesn't have others clamoring for their support, and I don't want to put Colin in the position of having to withdraw their support because I haven't held up my end of our agreement."

The beach was sparsely populated at this hour, offering a sense of solitude and privacy. The sounds were hushed, with only the gentle crashing of waves and the occasional call of a seabird breaking the silence. A spry eighty-something-year-old couple power walked past them.

He reached over and touched Arden's arm to get her attention. "What changed your mind about doing the interview?"

~

ARDEN KNEW it was a fair question. She had made such a big deal over saying "no," it was too much to hope her sudden reversal would fly beneath the radar. But how much to tell him?

Colin's words from their kitchen conversation kept looping through her head. No matter how hard she tried to shake them, she couldn't ignore the truth—her brother was right. Arden's efforts, which he'd called too passive, hadn't led to the success she'd hoped for. By now, she should have more than just one reservation booked. Other beach towns were already filling up for the summer.

If she weren't careful, she would prove her family right. Her bid for independence would collapse faster than a sandcastle at high tide. Their lips may not utter the words, "I told you so," but she'd hear them loud and clear.

But a television interview? Could she do that? Despite having told him she'd do it, the doubts wouldn't disappear. That insistent male voice from her past ricocheted inside her head.

*"Why are you so stiff on camera? As my wife, you need to do better."*

Her breath rushed up her throat, alongside the nausea.

Even if she could push through the anxiety, Nick would still be disappointed in her part of the interview. Lincoln always had been. Could she really face letting Nick down too? Seeing that same disappointment, the same quiet judgment she'd endured from her husband? How would she handle it?

Arden sighed before finally answering. "I'm in the process of turning my home and the lighthouse into a bed and breakfast. I've committed to having Keeper's Quarters ready for the spring Faith Works gala and the summer vacation season. Your nonprofit isn't the only one that could use the publicity."

"Why the hesitation then?" he asked, genuine curiosity in his eyes. "It seems like the interview would be an easy yes. Seeing you on TV would give Keeper's Quarters a face. Not some anonymous bed and breakfast."

That was the problem. She'd just as soon leave her face out of it.

Her expression must have reflected her inner struggle. Nick stood and took her hand, tugging her along beside him. "Let's take a walk."

His take-charge move annoyed and thrilled her at the same time.

As soon as they reached the water's edge, Nick released her hand. She missed its warmth.

He pushed his hands into the pockets of his track pants and focused his full attention on her. "Why don't you tell me the real reason you don't want to do this interview."

She tried to look away, but his gentle probing reached a place she wasn't sure she wanted to expose. A tingle spread through her chest. He saw her—really saw *her*. Not Lincoln's wife. Not Colin's little sister. Not John and Lila's daughter. Just Arden Gray. As if he genuinely wanted to get to know her, to connect with who she was beneath it all. Could she risk that? Was it wise to let him see just how broken she was?

Oh, the temptation. He was the first man who made her think beyond her lighthouse. Beyond her past relationship failures. For the first time, she wanted to share a bit of her burden. Nick brought that out in her. His kindness to Jonah, his support when she sobbed on his shoulder—she could almost see him as a soft place to land. Someone she could confide in without fear.

She swallowed, preparing to dip a toe in the proverbial water. "I'm not a fan of being in front of a camera."

Nick's smile was easy, no judgment in sight. "It's normal to feel nervous. Especially if you haven't done it before."

She laughed, with no humor to back it up. "Oh, I've been in front of cameras before, and it never went well."

His smile crept into a grin. "What happened? Did you trip?

Jumble your words?" His eyes widened. "Or did you open your mouth and nothing came out?"

She rolled her eyes. "Nothing so dramatic."

Arden twirled a finger around a curl as she allowed her mind to travel to the past.

"I'm not sure what was so bad, now that I think back on it, but my husband was clear how unacceptable my performance had been. Lincoln was head of a museum board and, as his wife, I chaired the women's auxiliary. A television station interviewed me when we opened an exhibit of a nationally recognized artist."

Arden gave up on the curl and pushed her hands through her hair.

"I thought it had gone well. Lincoln said I was unprofessional and clumsy. Next thing I knew, I was working with a beauty pageant coach so I wouldn't embarrass him again."

She risked a sideways glance and was gratified by the dumb-founded expression on Nick's face.

He moved his head from side to side. "Seriously? That's even a thing? Your husband sounds like a real peach." He slanted her a sheepish look. "I'm sorry. I shouldn't have said that."

How utterly adorable. She chuckled. "That's okay."

He picked up a shell, examined it, and tossed it into the waves. "With all that training, I'm sure you'll be a pro."

Arden glanced at him from the corner of her eyes. "I didn't say I ever became good at it."

In fact, Lincoln had assured her she never had. But Nick didn't need to know that.

"I'm really too busy to mess with a television interview. Maybe this isn't such a good idea. I have so much to do. The clock is ticking, and I need to have the guest rooms ready before summer gets here."

Not to mention her parents. As sponsors of the Faith Works gala, they would be staying with her while in town. If she were to ever gain their respect, Keeper's Quarters had to be top notch.

Nick laughed. "Oh no, you don't. I see what you're trying to do. I don't think an hour or so would make or break your timeline." He leaned toward her, bumping shoulders, and sent her a cocky grin. "You wouldn't deprive Jonah from his fifteen minutes of fame, would you?"

Arden admired his boyishly eager face, and her resistance headed out to sea with the wind. He reminded her of pre-Miley Liam Hemsworth. Who could resist that?

They had returned to the steps leading back to the lighthouse. She rubbed her hands up and down her arms to generate some warmth. She looked over her shoulder to where Nick followed a couple of steps behind her.

His furrowed brow suggested he was still thinking about the interview.

She stopped and turned at the top of the stairs, their difference in height erased as they faced each other eye-to-eye.

"Don't worry. I'll do the interview, but don't say I didn't warn you."

Nick reached out and tucked a blowing curl behind her ear. "Thank you. You won't regret it."

Arden sucked in a breath and resisted the urge to lean her cheek into his hand. She forced herself to turn away and mumbled, "I already do."

# CHAPTER 6

A couple of days later, Nick stood on Arden's porch, ringing the doorbell for the third time. Her SUV sat in the driveway. Why wasn't she answering?

Again, he pounded on the door.

It finally opened, with Arden glaring at him from across the threshold.

He pressed his lips together. Given the daggers flying from her eyes and the scowl twisting her lips, he knew she would not thank him for laughing out loud.

Unruly blonde corkscrews stuck out every which way, defying the bandana headband and ponytail. She was in what he figured to be her DIY clothes based on their condition. Some sort of residue had dried on her cheeks, forearms, and t-shirt, but not a speck of makeup.

She tilted her chin as if she dared him to comment.

He could tell her she looked adorable but knew better. However, the grin could only remain hidden for so long before it broke loose. "Hey there, beautiful. Someone was eager to come home."

Nick took out the rudely awakened Jonah from beneath his

jacket.

His fur was rumpled from being stuffed inside the jacket, and his mood matched his bed-headed ear fur.

Just like that, both the woman's scowl and the dog's grumpiness evaporated.

Arden reached for Jonah before the words had left his mouth.

The dog wiggled out of Nick's arms, his ill humor forgotten.

"Hey there, baby." Her eyes full of joy, she snuggled the dog and looked at Nick with hope in her gaze. "So, I can keep him? He's home for good?"

Nick nodded. "He's done well. His oxygen levels are on the low end of normal and his lungs have cleared enough not to be a danger. He can continue to improve at home." He pulled a pill bottle from his pocket.

"Give him this antibiotic every eight hours for ten days as a precaution. We'll do a follow-up chest X-ray in a couple of weeks, so you'll need to bring him back in. Stella has emailed you a feeding regimen, and I have a bag of prescription dog food in the truck. We need to beef this guy up."

Scratching Jonah under the chin, he added, "This is one lucky dude."

Jonah crawled from Arden's arms onto her shoulder, licking her ear.

She laughed and kissed his neck. "Stop. That tickles." She raised her face, the hint of happy tears made her eyes even brighter. "Thank you. I'm thrilled to have him home."

Nick grinned. "I think he's thrilled to be here."

Arden raised an eyebrow. "Is that your professional opinion?"

"Absolutely. I speak fluent dog." He shrugged. "As you might imagine, it comes in handy."

Silence settled between them. She rubbed her cheek against Jonah and warmth spread throughout Nick's body. A tide of affection for Arden flooded his chest, catching him off guard.

She murmured sweet nothings into Jonah's ear while Nick

waged a battle with his hands, denying the urge to pull them both into a hug.

Jonah whined, squirming for all he was worth. Jonah to the rescue.

Arden rolled her eyes. "I may not be fluent in dog-speak, but even I know he's asking for a potty break."

"Here, I'll take him with me while I get the dog food out of my truck." He took the dog from her arms and nodded toward her outfit. "It seems like we've interrupted your work."

She plucked at her t-shirt and pulled the bandana from her head. "I was upstairs waging war with some uncooperative wallpaper." She wiped what he now could identify as dried paste from her face.

After a quick trip to his truck, he followed her through the open door with the bag of food under one arm, Jonah under the other.

Jonah wiggled to be set free, and they watched him tip toe down the hallway, his nose working overtime. The soft click of his nails on the hardwood made them both smile.

Jonah continued into the kitchen, a bit of confidence lending a swagger to his miniature steps. Nick and Arden followed the pint-sized wiggle as he sniffed his way to the wire crate Arden had set up for him, complete with a comfy bed Nick wouldn't mind sleeping on.

Proceeding inside, Jonah turned three circles to the right, dug into the blankets, then turned three circles to the left. Dug some more. He curled up like a pinwheel and gave an inordinately loud sigh for such a small dog.

They laughed.

Nick squatted to pet Jonah, then latched the door. "The excitement seems to have caught up with him. It will be some time before he recovers his stamina."

Nick and Arden stood side-by-side, watching Jonah sleep as if they had just put their child to bed.

*Whoa.*

He brought that train of thought to a screeching halt. The domesticity of this moment triggered an alarm inside his brain. No wife. No children. Not for a very long time. If ever.

Arden wiped her hands down her leggings and turned toward the fridge. She removed bottled water for him and a Diet Coke for herself. She then pulled out a stool from the island and sat down. "Did you happen to catch the news last night?" She paid inordinate attention to the opening of a soda bottle. Something was up.

He took a deep pull from the water bottle. "No. Dr. Weston called me in to assist with an emergency surgery." Noticing her raised eyebrow, he added, "Beagle chewed a battalion of toy army men. But he's good now."

"Well, I don't make a habit of watching the news, but I needed some background noise as I stripped wallpaper. Tiffany didn't waste any time before airing a trailer for our upcoming interview."

His turn to raise a brow. "Wow. I just let her know yesterday afternoon that we agreed to do it."

"Maybe she's afraid we'll change our mind. Looks like she pieced something together from her cell phone video from that morning." She pulled out her own phone and tapped away. "Here. She posted it to social media."

Nick moved to stand behind her, looking over her shoulder. His nose was inches from her hair. He inhaled her fresh scent. Coconut shampoo. Nice.

Arden pressed the play arrow, and he relived Jonah's rescue through the raw video footage. The video began with Arden rushing into the waves, a testament to her compassion and courage.

Nick's heart swelled as he watched Arden's gentle yet firm grasp on the frightened canine, cradling him in her arms like a precious treasure. Her actions revealed more than just a woman saving a dog. They demonstrated a determined and capable individual, showcasing her innate kindness and readiness to confront challenges head-on.

His admiration for her deepened, and he found himself captivated by the way she transformed a potentially dire situation into an act of remarkable compassion.

Next, he saw himself enter the frame, running in to offer help. He remembered how out of breath he had been, eager to help both woman and dog.

Professional instinct analyzed the critical care he provided the animal. He saw nothing he'd do differently.

Arden turned toward the cell phone lens, then rushed behind him up the stairs, which is where the video ended.

Arden looked up at him, their faces too close for comfort.

Nick stepped back and ran a hand through his hair.

Her frown and narrowed eyes told him she was expecting some sort of reaction.

"Can you play it again?" This time he focused on Tiffany's voiceover.

*"A heartwarming tale unfolds as a small dog's life is snatched from the clutches of the ocean's embrace, all thanks to the valiant efforts of Good Samaritans, Arden Gray and Dr. Nick Monroe. But this story is about more than just a rescue; it's a journey of compassion and connection. And speaking of connection, our sources suggest a romance might be blossoming amidst the waves. Join us for an in-depth look at the faces behind this heroic act. Coming soon."*

"Wow." Nick's mind scrambled for something to say, but Arden didn't wait for his wits to return.

"This is all your fault. I told you that letting her think we're an item was a mistake." Her mouth tightened after her clipped words.

"I already apologized." He scraped his hand across his face. "The fact still remains we'll both benefit from this. I'm sure the relationship thing will blow over. We'll just focus on Jonah during the interview."

Arden left her chair to toss her Diet Coke bottle into the recycle bin. Storm clouds gathered across her face. But instead of the thunder and lightning she'd shown him before, this was more like fog and shadow.

He swallowed, hating to think he put that sadness there. He gentled his voice. "Is it really so bad if people think we're seeing each other?"

She looked him straight in the eye. "Yeah. It is."

His throat continued to close—no amount of swallowing would ease this unexpected ache. He nodded, lips thinning. "How can I make this situation better? Do you want me to tell Tiffany the truth? That we're just friends?" He cocked his head. "We are friends, right?"

She sighed and looked off to the side where Jonah softly snored. "Yes. But confronting Tiffany with the truth will come across as if we're trying to hide something. You know...protesting too much and all that."

Taking that as a win, Nick shifted his attention to the front door before their truce had a chance to deteriorate. "I better head back to the clinic." He tipped his chin toward a sleeping Jonah. "Our little friend has settled in nicely."

Arden followed him to the door. "Thank you for bringing him home." She laid her hand on his arm for a fleeting moment. "I do appreciate all you've done."

"No problem. It's what I do." He winked, flashing a grin. She didn't need to know he'd never personally delivered a patient home before.

Pushing aside the nagging thought that being around Arden might lead to more firsts, he reminded himself—it didn't matter. He wouldn't be in town long enough for it to matter.

~

A FEW DAYS LATER, Arden opened her front door to find Nick balancing a couple of pizza boxes from Rosario's on one forearm, while several bulging plastic bags dangled from his other hand. The warm scent of yeast and oregano floated into her foyer. His tousled golden hair and the rumpled t-shirt and jeans made him almost as appetizing as the promise of gooey cheese and spicy pepperoni.

She noticed the suitcase and shopping bags at his feet. She tried to make sense of the puzzle standing on her front porch. Her furrowed brow and narrowed gaze must have displayed her confusion.

With a sheepish grin, he said, "I'll let Colin explain. Just remember, I come bearing gifts."

Her brother climbed the steps, loaded down with shopping bags and a dog bed. "If you're the one bearing gifts, why am I the one carting them from the car?"

Arden stood in stunned silence, her gaze fixed on the chaotic back-and-forth of the two men making three more trips to the car. Each. The pile of bags from Pets-R-Us was bad enough, but all this luggage suggested a much more alarming scenario.

*This must be some sort of practical joke, right?* They can't actually be moving in. "Colin, what on earth are you doing?"

"Sorry I didn't call ahead, but I wanted to surprise you." He turned on the puppy-dog eyes. "Surprise..." His voice was weak and petered into nothing toward the end.

Nick stepped in. "What Colin means to say is that we're homeless."

"Not homeless," Colin corrected. "Temporarily displaced. I was in Charlotte all day and Nick was at the clinic. While we were gone, an upstairs pipe burst, flooding the house. There's no way we can stay there tonight. The insurance guy comes out tomorrow to let us know what we're up against as far as repairs."

"Colin, you know there's only one livable bedroom here, and

it's already taken. By me." Keeper's Quarters was in no shape to open its doors to uninvited guests.

"Our sleeping bags and cots are still in the car so we can bunk upstairs. You won't even know we're here."

"I've lived with you before. I know better."

Colin went back, presumably to grab even more stuff.

She rubbed an ache from her forehead and motioned to the shopping bags. "What's all this?"

Nick shrugged. "Gifts for Jonah. I thought I could pick up some items for you since he's your first dog. It's the least I can do. Especially now since I'm invading your space."

Great. Nice as well as handsome. She had quite the job cut out for her if she intended to keep her distance—both emotional and physical. "That was very thoughtful."

Her foyer seemed to shrink with him in the space. Arden didn't know what to do with the sudden awkwardness between them. Granted, awkwardness was often her middle name, as she had demonstrated when she'd blubbered into his shirt after rescuing Jonah. But she had worked past that. For the most part anyway.

She and Nick would be under the same roof. Arden did not have the time, nor the emotional fortitude, to deal with having him so close. How was she to maintain her distance? She was drawn to him in ways she had never been drawn to any other man. Including her husband.

Arden glanced at Nick, her heart fluttering as her eyes met his.

The eye contact lasted for only a heartbeat before he cleared his throat. "I'll just put the food on the counter."

As she watched him head into the kitchen, Arden fiddled with the edge of her shirt. She had barely gotten a handle on ok teaming up with him for the interview. But this new context— the intimacy of sharing a living space—stirred a mix of emotions she had no desire to confront.

Nick returned to the foyer as Colin came banging through the door, dropping two cots, sleeping bags, and who knew what else at Nick's feet.

"I've brought everything this far. You take them upstairs."

Nick gathered a load and left. Hopefully he didn't hear her sigh of relief.

Colin turned to her. "Den, I'm sorry to intrude like this, but I wasn't sure where else to go on such short notice."

Arden rolled her eyes. She put her arm around him and guided him into the kitchen. "It's okay. Family intrudes and family gets over it."

# CHAPTER 7

If it weren't for the lighthouse behind her and Jonah at the end of a leash, Nick would think he had turned into the wrong driveway. But no, his heart rate picked up at the sight of her, so it could only be Arden.

The woman walking toward him was wearing black trousers and a flowy white shirt type thing. And fancy high heels. Which would be fine if she were heading to a business meeting. But a walk on the beach? Nick didn't spare many thoughts for fashion practicalities, but even he knew this wasn't a good idea.

The real travesty was how her hair was tamed into submission. He could all but hear the strands screaming for release. Instead, it was knotted tight at the base of Arden's neck. Such a shame.

He bent down to give Jonah a welcome scratch then looked up at Arden. "Is that what you're wearing for the interview?" Even before her lips tightened into a straight line, Nick grimaced.

But instead of the sharp retort he expected, a shadow shaded her eyes. "It's appropriate for a television interview, don't you think?" She straightened her cuffs, not meeting his eyes. "I have done this before, and have been trained accordingly, remember?"

Ah, yes. The pageant coach.

Has she no idea how adorable she is? Even in her self-consciousness—or maybe because of it—all he wanted to do was wrap her in a hug and reassure her she was perfect just as God had created her. She had told him enough about her poor excuse of a late husband that he knew she was battling some internal script on a never-ending loop.

Before he could respond, the news van pulled in and Tiffany hopped out as the driver began unloading video equipment.

Jonah barked, daring anyone to come close. Big bark. Small dog. Didn't matter.

Arden scooped Jonah into her arms and shushed him. But the little dog didn't miss a beat.

Nick wasn't sure how Arden had kept her balance on those heels. Or kept her hearing, for that matter, with the barking up against her ear.

"Hush, Jonah. It's okay."

Jonah licked Arden's cheek, then throttled back to a low growl.

They exchanged greetings with Tiffany and met her cameraman, Joe.

Tiffany turned her attention to Arden, considering her from head to toe. "I'm sorry, Arden. My assistant should have informed you I wanted to conduct the interview on the beach. If you're quick, we may have time for you to change clothes." She dropped her gaze. "And shoes."

Nick watched as pink spread across Arden's face. A mask that had nothing to do with makeup came down.

She straightened, standing extra tall, and turned Jonah over to him. "I won't be long."

It was Nick's turn for Tiffany's professional once over. She took in his jeans and black long-sleeved buttoned-down shirt sporting the Vets Without Boundaries logo. He must have passed inspection since she didn't send him inside.

"How are you finding Beacon Bluff? It's not terribly exciting during the off season."

"I'm enjoying my visit. I spend most of my time helping Doc Weston in the clinic and working to establish my mission."

"And, of course, there's your time with Arden." Tiffany smiled.

"Of course." Nick was glad Arden wasn't here for that comment. She was nervous enough without introducing comments of a fictional relationship.

"Did you say mission?" She lifted her chin toward his shirt. "Vets Without Boundaries? Tell me about it."

*Thank you, Lord, for a reporter's curiosity.*

By the time he had explained the concept of Vets Without Boundaries and answered her questions, Arden had rejoined them.

This time, she wore black jeans, rolled at the ankle, and had exchanged the heels for black slip-ons. She hadn't changed the white top, and her hair was still imprisoned at the back of her neck.

Tiffany motioned to the path leading to the beach. "Shall we?" She walked on ahead, discussing interview logistics with Joe.

Nick and Arden followed, Jonah trotting along beside them.

Nick studied Arden from the corner of his eye, observing the tense set of her shoulders and the vee between her brows. Her breathing was shallow, and she had caught her bottom lip between her teeth.

He had clearly underestimated the amount of anxiety this interview would cause. He reached for her hand, not put off by the slight tremble. "It's okay. You'll be terrific."

"And you're sure of this how?"

"Because you love Jonah. This is his story, not ours."

They had come to a stop, turning to face one another.

Nick gave her hand a squeeze. He looked down to where Jonah sniffed clumps of sea grass. "He was brave and beat the odds. I have every confidence you'll be able to do the same."

"Thank you, Nick." She then rushed ahead, calling for Jonah to keep up.

His two-inch legs churned to meet the challenge.

Once they reached the shore, Tiffany took charge. She turned them so they weren't looking into the sun, keeping the ocean at their back. She instructed Arden to pick up Jonah, then turned to Joe. Morphing into her on-camera persona, Tiffany nodded for the cameraman to begin rolling.

Nick barely registered the bright voice welcoming future viewers. Instead, his focus was on the woman standing beside him. They weren't touching, but he felt her body tense as soon as she noticed the camera's red light. Arden's smile was practiced, but stiff. Her hands still, but clenched.

Tiffany launched into her introduction. "Last Thursday's storm brought more than heavy rain and flash flooding to Beacon Bluff. It also brought a struggling dog to shore, at the brink of death. We're talking today with the two Good Samaritans who found him and saved his life. First, let's meet the little guy who has lived to tell his tale."

As if on cue, Jonah licked Arden's cheek, then turned his head to face the camera. This pup was born for the spotlight.

Tiffany directed her questions to Arden, artfully turning her body to the camera in much the same way spokesmodels hawk used cars. Not an unflattering angle in sight.

Arden, on the other hand, straightened her posture and faced the camera head-on—jaw set, eyes narrowed, shoulders back.

"So, Arden, who do we have here? Can you introduce us to your friend?"

Smiling tightly, she answered, "This is Jonah."

When nothing more was forthcoming, Tiffany stepped in. "And how did you happen to find him, and what shape was he in?"

"I was out for an early morning walk on the beach and saw him struggling in the waves. I could tell he needed help, since he was gasping for air." She nodded to Nick. "Nick was jogging on the beach at the time when Jonah needed him most."

That gave Tiffany the opportunity to shift attention to him.

He answered her questions, relaying the story of Jonah's rescue. Wrapping it up, he said, "Jonah found his guardian angel that morning. If it wasn't for Arden, I'm afraid he would have become a sad casualty."

He reached over and scratched Jonah under the chin, causing the dog to moan his approval.

Arden looked up, meeting his eye, and they both chuckled.

Jonah scrambled out of Arden's arms, trying to reach Nick.

Arden was forced to move closer so the dog wouldn't fall.

Jonah rested his two front paws on Nick's bicep while the rest of his long body rested in Arden's arms. Jonah turned to the camera, tongue sticking out as if he were giving the audience a big smile.

Tiffany laughed. "Well, it seems that Jonah has claimed you both. For viewers who aren't aware, Arden owns our local lighthouse and is in the process of renovating it. Won't you tell us what you have in mind for our beloved landmark?"

"I'm happy to. Keeper's Quarters will open this summer as a bed and breakfast. We'll also feature a museum inside the lighthouse, displaying some artifacts and highlighting its history."

Tiffany turned to the camera. "Hopefully those in our viewing audience will consider Keeper's Quarters for their next beach vacation. Beacon Bluff may have taken a hit from Hurricane Camilla, but it's back in business."

Arden's smile lit up her face. "Our doors will be open, and Jonah will be waiting to say hello."

"Nick, I understand you are launching an organization to help animals in need. Please fill us in on your efforts."

"Actually, Tiffany, I'm launching a veterinarian ministry in Honduras that educates folks on caring for their animals and livestock so they can avoid disease. As you can imagine, rabies can wreak havoc on a small village, as well as other health-related dangers."

"If any of our viewers wish to learn more, where can they go?"

Nick glanced over at Arden. "I can't speak for Keeper's Quarters, but viewers can find Vets Without Boundaries on our website or on any social media platform."

"Same for Keeper's Quarters. We're taking reservations now."

Tired of being ignored, Jonah barked, issuing his own invitation.

The humans laughed and Arden set him down on the sand.

"There you have it. Just as Jonah fought his way back to life, so too is the humble beach town of Beacon Bluff after Hurricane Camilla. Like our beloved lighthouse, his rescue demonstrates hope and proves there is still good in this world. That's all for now. I'm Tiffany Meyer, reporting for Coastal News Now."

"Cut!" Tiffany stowed her microphone back into its protective case. "Joe, let's get some promo footage of these three walking the beach. We'll want to get the lighthouse in the background and a close up of Nick's shirt with his ministry's logo."

Nick handed Jonah over to Arden and reached to shake Tiffany's hand. "Thank you for working Vets Without Boundaries into the piece."

Arden smiled, and for the first time Nick thought it was genuine. "Yes, I can't thank you enough for highlighting Keeper's Quarters."

Tiffany shrugged. "I can't promise how much will make it through editing. Now you guys take Jonah and walk toward the lighthouse so Joe can finish up. I'm heading back to the news van to check my messages. I will let you know when the piece is scheduled to air."

Tiffany trudged through the loose sand to the van, scrolling through her phone as she went.

Joe motioned down the beach, hefting the camera onto his shoulder. "After you."

Nick took off a few steps ahead, turning around to jog backwards. He called Jonah while Arden sat him down and unclipped his leash.

They both laughed as Jonah's little legs threw sand in his wake—taking at least two strides for their one.

Nick's heart stuttered as Arden jogged after the dog, strands of her hair breaking free from its prison.

Arden tripped and fell to the sand, but her laugh assured him all was well.

He rushed to her side but before he could help, Jonah pounced on top of her, licking her face. Nick took her hands and helped her to her feet but must have tugged too hard since she landed against his chest. He steadied her with a hand at her waist, their eyes meeting, both wider than normal. Aware of Joe and his video camera, Nick let her go.

Arden looked down, tucking that loose strand behind her ear then grabbed the dog, who was running circles around their legs. She jogged on ahead, laughing over her shoulder.

He followed, shortening his stride so he could extend the game. Her laugh caught the wind and flew back to him. Reaching the boulders that protected the base of the lighthouse from erosion, they pulled up short.

Joe wasn't far behind, keeping the lens trained on them as they returned to the lighthouse.

Jonah danced around their feet, yipping, urging them to continue their game.

Nick could only imagine the picture they must make. His throat tightened. He refused to cast himself in the role of family. Maybe someday, when he had completed the work he'd been called to do. Maybe someday he would open his heart again. Maybe someday when the risk of rejection was minimized.

But someday wasn't today.

∼

"Good morning."

Arden yelped. She juggled her wallet, the bag holding her chocolate-iced donut, and the large to-go cup of Diet Coke.

The Lamplighter was bustling with the morning crowd, and she hadn't heard Nick's approach.

After gathering herself, she turned toward the voice responsible for her clumsiness. "Good morning, Nick. Trying to catch the worm?" Arden winced. With that riveting conversation starter, she sounded just like her dad.

He thought for a moment. "No worms, but I did get up earlier than usual for my run. Thought I'd reward myself with soy milk in my coffee this morning." He nodded his thanks towards Madge, who winked at him as she set the paper cup in front of him.

"Woohoo! Arden! Over here!"

She turned, along with everyone else in the diner.

Bea Mallory waved her to the table where she and her friend, Ivey Swain, were sitting.

Arden turned to Nick. "I better head over there. She won't settle down until I do." Before she walked off, Arden wagged her finger toward his coffee cup. "Be careful. I hear that fake milk is the gateway to the real thing."

The older woman stood and called out again, interrupting Nick's chuckle. "And bring that fine friend of yours over here with you."

Groaning, Arden spoke over her shoulder. "Join me at your own risk."

"How bad can it be? Lead the way."

Giving Bea and Miss Ivey quick hugs, she introduced Nick. "He's working with Colin on a project with H3."

Bea pointed to two available chairs at the table. "Both of you. Sit."

And they did. No questions asked.

Bea frowned and crossed her arms, pinning Nick with a glare, rivaling any self-respecting drill sergeant. "Rumor has it you're shacking up with my girl here. What do you have to say for yourself?"

Arden winced. "Bea! Nobody is shacking up with anyone. Please keep your voice down."

Bea Mallory wasn't known for her subtlety. From the top of her pixie-cut salt and pepper hair, down past her Elton John glasses and faux Liz Taylor jewelry, the *grande dame* of Beacon Bluff commanded attention like none other.

Miss Ivey glanced up from the pile of yarn in her lap, raising an eyebrow. The frantic click of her knitting needles spoke volumes.

Ivey Swain was the perfect foil for Bea's flamboyance. Where Bea wore purple and red, Ivey wore lilac and rose. Bea's hair was cropped short, but Ivey's luxurious white hair flowed to her shoulders, held back with a velvet ribbon. The top of Ivey's head may only reach Bea's shoulders, but her Southern grace made sure she stood out in a crowd. Bea enjoyed being noticed. Miss Ivey, not so much.

Nick cleared his throat. "Ladies, can I get you anything? Tea? A muffin, maybe?"

Bea leveled him with a stare and crossed her arms. "You can't buy us with your pretty manners. What's this I hear about you two being an item? We've known this young'un since she was knee high to a seagull. You mind your manners, or you'll be answering to us."

Miss Ivey paused to shake the pointy end of a needle at Nick.

Arden sat down and removed her chocolate donut from its takeout bag. "Now ladies, there's no need to get huffy. No shacking up. I promise. He and Colin are staying with me until the house is repaired. I'm sure you've heard about the water damage."

"Of course I have. Arlis, with Coastal Insurance, told his wife, who told Cindy at the Food Lion, who plays Uno every Thursday with Dr. Weston's wife." Bea smiled, basking in the pride of her incomparable network of informants.

"Then you also know Colin is staying as well. The boys are upstairs and I'm downstairs."

"Girl, it's not you I'm worried about." Bea returned her laser focus to Nick. "Young man, Arden is a good girl. Been through enough trouble without you adding to it."

"Ma'am, I respect her too much to cause her or her reputation harm." He crossed his fingers over his heart. "Scout's honor." Nick's earnest gaze and sincere smile belied his casual words, causing Bea to relax her shoulders and uncross her arms.

"Well, are you an item or not?" The growl may be gone, but the demand remained. "I saw that interview on TV and it sure looked like it."

Arden exchanged a glance with Nick, complete with one raised eyebrow. This was the moment of truth. Were they going forward with this charade? Or not?

Nick put an arm around the back of Arden's chair. "Who could resist?"

Oh, he was good. She admired his non-answer, avoiding an outright lie.

"I figured. Just remember. We've got our eyes on you." Bea narrowed her eyes, daring Nick to step out of line.

Heat spread across Arden's cheeks, and embarrassment brought a sheen to her brow. Last night, she had viewed the TV screen between open fingers—wanting to watch, yet afraid of what she'd see. She had been right to be scared. What she saw was a stiff, talking mannequin who had no place beside such a vibrant man and adorable dog.

A draft of chilled air hit Arden in the back. Glancing over her shoulder, she saw Tiffany barreling through the door and heading toward them.

There wasn't enough Diet Coke in the universe to fortify her for the reporter's morning effervescence.

"Glad I ran into the two of you. It saves me time later." Tiffany pulled out the remaining empty chair. "Miss Bea, Miss Ivey. Good to see you both."

Bea raised her coffee cup in a toast before taking a sip, and Miss Ivey looked up from her knitting and smiled.

Tiffany motioned to Madge for a cup of coffee, then turned her attention to Arden and Nick. "Did you two see last night's segment? Our viewer response has been through the roof. But as cute as Jonah is, it's been all about #Arick."

Nick took a sip of his coffee. "Hashtag what?"

"A-R-I-C-K. It's called a ship name." Tiffany explained.

"As in relationship?" He shook his head. "I'm getting old."

Tiffany ignored him. "You may have heard that the Beacon Bluff Humane Society is sponsoring an Empty the Shelter event."

Nick nodded. "Yes, we got something about it in the mail at the office."

"Probably asking for a donation. I'm on their board and we're hoping to find homes for every animal in residence. A big undertaking, let me tell you. We still have so many cats and dogs left behind from Camilla."

Arden sighed. "I hope it's a success. My heart aches for those poor babies."

"You can do more than wish us well. The board would love #Arick to judge the rescue dog show. There are several activities planned, but that's the main event."

Nick cocked an eyebrow in her direction. "I'm game. What about you, Arden?"

Arden frowned. She had hoped to keep this so-called relationship more on the downlow. "As much as I would like to, my to-do list hasn't gotten much shorter since you asked me to do the interview. I'm on a tight schedule to get Keeper's Quarter's ready for summer." She quirked an eyebrow at him. "Especially since I now have two unexpected house guests."

Tiffany sat back in her chair and crossed her arms. "I have

heard that one item near the top of that list is securing reservations for the summer. Word on the street is that you've only booked one room for the entire season."

Whose word on what street? A cleared throat and sudden rummaging through a pocketbook caused Arden to close her eyes with a soft sigh. Bea.

It seemed that network of hers worked both ways. Combined with Tiffany's reporter instinct, Arden wouldn't be surprised if they knew what shampoo she used.

Arden's flushed face warmed her all the way to her toes. "There's still time."

Tiffany shrugged. "Maybe. But why not speed up the process by raising your visibility? Coastal News Now's viewership reaches the entire Southeast."

As much as she hated going back in front of a camera, Arden couldn't dispute the facts. All her hard work wouldn't matter if she didn't get any reservations. If Keeper's Quarters didn't enjoy a profitable summer, how much longer would she be able to avoid her family's pressure to join H3? Her need for the bed and breakfast to succeed far exceeded her stage fright.

She looked at Nick. At least she wouldn't be doing it alone. It had amazed Arden at how relaxed she had been while they played on the beach after the interview. Nick was so much fun to be around. Maybe it would rub off on her again.

While she was being honest with herself, she may as well admit she enjoyed being around him for more than his good humor. Something about him made her heart stir to life. Made her female instincts perk up their ears.

But she still had her reservations—regarding both the dog show and Nick Monroe.

"What would it involve?"

"Not a purebred in sight. The categories are Best Couch Potato, Best Einstein Look-a-like, that sort of thing. Of course, Jonah is invited as well."

Nick laughed. "That's a dog show I can support." He looked at Arden. "What if I help you? I'm quite handy, you know." He grinned, wiggling his eyebrows.

Not one to remain silent for long, Bea announced, "I think it's a splendid idea." She slapped the table, pronouncing her approval. She shot him a deliberate look. "Idle hands are the devil's workshop."

"Arden, dear, think of the fun you'd have." Miss Ivey was becoming downright talkative.

Nick's fingers rotated his to-go cup before looking Arden in the eye. "You know as well as I do that the competition is fierce for this grant. Since I've spent my life moving around, I don't have any community ties to speak of. This would go a long way toward improving that."

Tiffany chimed in. "You and Nick wouldn't be the only attraction. Jonah is quite the celebrity in his own right. The fact that he himself is a rescue, I'm sure would encourage others to look closer at the animals inside our kennels. Those dogs deserve a loving home just as Jonah does, don't you think?"

Arden's shoulders slumped, and she heaved a sigh. She wasn't going to win this. "That's fighting dirty, Tiffany."

Tiffany grinned. "Does it work?"

Arden rotated her head to ease some tension, then shot Nick a look. "Can you repair drywall?"

# CHAPTER 8

After snapping Jonah's leash onto his collar, Arden made quick work of heading to the beach and sitting on her favorite step. She marveled at the unseasonably mild winter weather, though, she would have been out here even if it were colder. But she was happy to wear fewer layers of clothing.

Jonah stretched out on the step below her, basking in the sunshine. His ribs had become less prominent. Another thing to be thankful for.

The pinging of her cell phone woke Jonah from his nap, and his side eye let her know he didn't appreciate the interruption.

Glancing at the caller ID, Arden rushed to answer. "Hi, Mom. How are you?"

"Hello, darling. I hope I'm not catching you at a bad time. I had a break in my day and wanted to touch base." Mom's soft Southern voice traveled loud and clear from Honduras, wrapping Arden in a tight maternal hug.

"Not at all. I'm sitting next—"

Rushing on before Arden finished speaking, Lila continued. "Your father and I are hosting a group of pastors and their wives from the States. I'm presenting our women's health initiative to the ladies while your dad takes the men into nearby villages to deliver food and pray with some families."

Arden could visualize her mother's animated features and hand gestures. Lila Bennet always bloomed wherever she was planted—even if it was 2,782 miles away from her only daughter.

"I know you and Daddy will inspire the living daylights out of those folks. Have you spoken with Colin? Have you heard about the damage to the house? The offices are ruined."

"Yes, the flood damage sounds just awful. I'm so glad you're there to help. Especially since Nick is staying with him for a bit. You're such a blessing, Arden. I only wish you would bless us here in Honduras."

Well, that hadn't taken long.

"Mom, we've been over this before. Honduras is your ministry, not mine."

"It could be. The Lord works in mysterious ways, darling. Only He can make your husband dying in a car wreck work out for good. And that good can lead you here to *Pena Blanca*."

Jonah heaved a giant sigh that was loud enough to be heard in Honduras.

"Did you say something, Arden? You're not still crying over Lincoln, are you?" The distance between them couldn't muffle the accusation.

"No, Mom, that's my dog, Jonah."

"That's right. Colin mentioned him." Something else that wasn't muffled—Mom's disapproval.

"He's the sweetest thing. I'll text you a picture. You'll get to meet him when you and Dad are here for the Faith Works gala."

"Darling, I'm sure he's cute as a button, but you shouldn't tie yourself down with a dog. Can't you find someone else to take him?"

"Why would I do that? I live alone, so he's good company. At least, I do when I'm not providing shelter for a displaced brother and his friend."

"There's no need to live alone. We have a cottage ready for you on the H3 campus. Of course, it would be problematic bringing a dog, what with permits, quarantine, and all. Besides, you would have all the company you need right here with us. In fact, you could travel with Nick. I hear there's been two cases of rabies reported several villages over."

"I have a business to get up and running and hopefully, with guests coming in, I won't be alone very often." Her comment was met with silence. Why had she hoped for something more? She knew better. "Mom, I need to run. Don't you need to get ready for your ladies' group?"

"You're right! What was I thinking? I want to look over my notes before the next session. It's so important that this goes well. We can help a lot of marginalized women if these ladies take this ministry back to their home churches."

Just like that, Mom's attention turned from her daughter to the ministry at hand. That particular diversion technique had served Arden well over the years. "They won't be able to resist you, Mom. Love you."

Arden ended the call, juggling the conflicting emotions that always followed a conversation with her mother.

Nick came down the stairs, dressed for a run. He glanced her way. "Everything okay?"

"Hmm? Oh, yes. Just talking with my mom. She's got a big conference today."

Jonah lifted his head and stretched, his scrawny body easing into the downward dog.

Nick turned his orange ball cap backward on his head. "I'm heading to the beach. Care to come? We can walk for a bit."

Arden answered with a simple shrug, but stood and began walking by his side. Her mind was still in Honduras.

Jonah dodged in and out from between their feet, avoiding the waves lapping onto the shore. The leash Arden held didn't allow him to venture far, although he did his best to pull her further into the loose sand.

Nick scooped him up and tucked him under an arm, eliminating the four-pawed tripping hazard. "Is everything okay in Honduras? You seem bothered."

She stopped dead in her tracks. "I am bothered. I can't even enjoy talking with my mother without her hounding me to join H3. I am 26 years old. I've essentially been on my own since I was seventeen when they left for Honduras. I can't imagine why she should be so concerned now."

"You were only seventeen? Who did you live with?" Nick came to a stop, turning toward her.

"The Gray family." At his quizzical look, she continued. "Yes, same last name as mine. They're my late husband's family."

"Is that how you met him?"

"No, our families had been close for years. They served senior leadership roles in my dad's church. Since Lincoln was several years older, we didn't hang in the same circles. Long story short? One day I was no longer the daughter of his parents' friends, and the next thing I knew I was the woman he wanted to marry." Arden didn't add that Lincoln's charm and good looks had once seemed like the cure for her overwhelming sadness. From the way Nick's gaze narrowed, she figured she didn't have to.

He considered Jonah, a frown marring his forehead. "It sounds as if a lot happened between Point A and Point B of your long story made short."

She shrugged. "It was a learning experience for sure."

An uncomfortable silence fell between them as they continued down the beach.

Arden took Jonah from Nick and set him down on the loose sand. "Let's see if this guy is ready to get his paws wet."

When Arden tugged the leash toward the water, Jonah plopped his hind end down and braced his front paws. If a dog could set his jaw, that's what she saw on Jonah's face.

She gently pulled him along, but all that did was create a long skid mark.

"I guess it's a bit too soon for him to jump right back into the water." Nick's lips were talking about the dog, but his eyes were speaking to her.

Arden nodded, her eyes holding his gaze for a moment. "Yes, it is." Picking up Jonah, she turned to retrace their steps to the lighthouse. "If it's okay with you, I'd like to head back."

"Sure. I'll see you back at the house after my run."

She knew he watched her until she reached the top of the stairs. Arden's sigh caught on a gust of wind. Maybe someday she'd dip her toes back into the water. If so, it would be with someone who wouldn't leave her for Honduras.

NICK WHISTLED. "This place is still a mess." He and Colin stood in what used to be Colin's home office. Nick could see where the flooding had left its mark on the walls, several inches above the warped hardwood floor. The earthy odor of germinating mold made his skin itch.

"Thanks, Captain Obvious." Colin's hands rested on his hips, and he kicked at some ceiling plaster that had been strewn across the floor. "It's going to be a while before we can move back in. Apparently, this disaster is just a sneak peek of what's ahead if we don't replace the entire plumbing system."

"I hate to hear that." Since not only was this Colin's home but also H3's stateside headquarters. Nick regretted the financial hit the ministry would take. Less money to go toward helping the people of Honduras.

*More time living under the same roof as Arden.*

He walked around the room, shaking his head to erase that ridiculous notion. He could feel Colin's stare stabbing between his shoulder blades.

With nothing more to say about their surroundings, tension strained between them.

Colin cleared his throat and shoved his hands into his back pockets. "There are no hard feelings, right? I know you were disappointed during the status call with Dad yesterday."

Nick widened his stance and crossed his arms. "I may be disappointed, but that doesn't mean I have hard feelings. I understand H3's position on not increasing the amount of money committed to Vets Without Boundaries. The only way you can continue to help people in Honduras is if you guard your financial health."

"It isn't that we don't believe in you or value your ministry. If it were solely up to Dad and me, the answer may have been different. But we knew it wouldn't fly with our board of directors."

"You don't need to explain. I'll figure something out." And Nick meant it. They couldn't continue helping people if they weren't fiscally responsible. "But speaking of hard feelings, you swiped the last helping of eggplant parmesan last night. That will take some getting over."

"When it comes to my sister's cooking, it's every man for himself." Colin's wide smile matched Nick's. Colin tossed Nick a bottle of water from the nearby cooler and took a long swallow from his own. "So, do I need to ask about your intentions regarding my sister?"

"Um...about that..."

Had Arden clued her brother in to their situation? If not, Nick knew he needed to warn Colin about the presumed relationship before any rumors reached his ears. Colin had never liked surprises.

"You may, or may not, hear that she and I are dating." He braced himself. Nick knew his friend had a prodigal past. He had respected Colin's privacy and never pressed for details, but he suspected Colin had used his muscles for more than lifting weights.

Colin's eyes froze into ice chips. "Do tell."

Nick raised an eyebrow. "No need to go all WWE. It concerns helping Vets Without Boundaries attract more funding." He filled Colin in on Faith Works' community preferences, Tiffany's request for an interview, her assumption of a relationship, and Arden's agreement to help him out.

"So, you see, not only will it help me become more visible in the community, but it will also help Arden launch her bed and breakfast."

Colin eased his stance, but his jaw could still crush walnuts. "I've noticed how you watch Arden when you think no one's looking. I see how you're quick to help with the dishes. Dude, I've lived with you, so I know that's not your go-to move."

"I'm not going to deny I like spending time with her. But that's it. There would be something wrong with me if I didn't, don't you think?"

Colin considered him for several moments, then looked down at the water bottle in his hand. "Look, man, be careful. She's been through a lot with that late husband of hers. The last thing she needs is to become involved, and then you take off for Honduras."

"I can only imagine what it must be like to lose a spouse."

"As far as I'm concerned, he did her a favor by flipping over that guardrail. It's everything that went on before that's the problem."

Nick straightened and forced his fists not to clench. "Did he hurt her?"

"Physically?" Anger hardened the face of his typically affable friend. "No. If he had, his health would have been at risk much sooner. That's all I'm going to say. If she wants you to know, she'll share it with you."

"Sounds like it's a personal story. Doubt I'll be around long enough to hear it." *Unfortunately.* Whoa. Where did that thought come from?

Colin took a seat on the edge of a still-damp wooden desk, and Nick didn't like the way his eyes narrowed. "You've changed after what happened with Vanessa. You don't stick around places, or people, for long."

A deep breath eased the tightness in his stomach, and he shrugged off the tension weighing on his shoulders. "Life lessons have a way of doing that."

With clarity that only distance can bring, Nick realized he was angrier with himself than with Vanessa. Sure, his younger, idealistic self had assumed that when she'd said she loved him, she'd meant it in a 'whither thou goest, I will go' kind of way.

Instead, her love had come with conditions. He should have seen it long before the ultimatum—an MBA candidate was never going to be happy caring for animals in a third-world country.

The ultimatum hadn't gone her way.

"Colin, even if I was tempted to play with Arden's emotions—which I'm not—I wouldn't disrespect our friendship that way. Besides, I would never risk H3's partnership with my clinic over romance. After watching my mom struggle through my dad's ministry, I have no intention of getting involved with anyone."

Colin stood and clapped Nick on the back. "I believe you. Just had to clear the air. Would've hated having to beat you to a pulp."

Nick chuckled. "Yeah, you and me both." He looked up at the gaping hole in the ceiling where the gushing water had done its worst. "Is it even safe to be in here?"

"The construction foreman did suggest we wear hard hats if we came back. Let's grab our stuff and get out of here."

Later, Nick sat on the scuffed hardwood floor of his room in Arden's home, back against the wall, computer on his lap. He had just finished sending emails, reviewing numbers from a veterinary supply company, and revising the clinic's start-up cost analysis. His mind now had plenty of space to reflect on his conversation with Colin.

Scenes from his time with Arden scrolled through his mind.

He saw her kneeling in the sand, compassion shining through the fear as she cared for a dying animal. Spitting mad when he'd interrupted her work.

Nick sat up straight, snapping himself out of the self-sabotaging train of thought. If he were a different man with a different mission, he could afford to explore the possibilities. But he wasn't. And he couldn't.

God had made him for the mission field. He had been born a pastor's kid—something he had in common with Arden. But where her family had prospered, and their ministry had financially flourished in Charlotte, Nick's parents were rural ministers. Their income had often included portions of the latest harvest or a side of grass-fed beef.

Not that he complained. The people they served were salt-of-the-earth folks, sincere in their affection and their faith. He had developed friendships with boys his age as they raced through corn fields, climbed hay bales, and had gotten sick from too many funnel cakes at the county fair. He may have been an only child, but he had a congregation full of siblings and adults he had considered family.

Until Dad got the call to move on down the road.

The first time it had happened, he had cried for weeks. The second, he had sulked for days. The third? He shrugged and got into the car.

God used his upbringing to prepare him for the transient life of a missionary. He wasn't a loner—far from it. He embraced people wherever he went and cared about their spiritual journey. He just didn't think of them as permanent fixtures. He'd never met a stranger but didn't have a lot of friends. He was happy taking his days—and his relationships—one at a time, with no eye toward the future.

Restless, he stood, stretched, and decided to head back to the beach. He had already completed his morning run. What's another couple of miles?

# CHAPTER 9

"*D*on't fail me now, you miserable hunk of metal." Arden repeatedly flicked the power switch on her stand mixer, hoping for a spark of life. The glass bowl was filled with flour, salt, proofed yeast, and water. In other words, goopy paste.

"That glare of yours is about to ship that mixer off to the island of misfit appliances. Can I help?"

Arden scowled at Nick. "Thing should have been trashed long ago."

Her mother had received the uglier-than-dirt avocado green stand mixer as a wedding gift. In a bout of sentimental weakness, Arden had rescued it from the donation bin.

Nick strolled to her side. "It won't turn on? You plugged it in, right?"

Her frustration turned toward Nick. "I'm not even going to answer that."

Nick grinned, but checked the outlet anyway. "What are you making? Or rather, what had you planned to make?"

Arden sighed, blowing a stray tendril of hair from her forehead. No matter how many hair ties she used, strands always escaped. Arden praised the day messy buns became a thing.

"I'm making bread to go with dinner tonight. Since you and Colin moved in, we've eaten nothing but fast food. I can appreciate a fine hamburger with fries—and often do—but I'm in the mood to cook."

Arden had always enjoyed making bread before her marriage, before Lincoln had deemed it unseemly. Plus, since coming to Beacon Bluff, she had discovered that some of her best ideas came while working in the kitchen. She had some logistics to work out concerning the lighthouse renovation, so she'd hauled out this monster and got to work.

She shot him a sly look. "I also figured you'd met your lifetime quota of saturated fats, so I'm going for something a bit healthier."

"You won't get any argument from me, although the thought of homemade bread smothered in butter suggests otherwise."

She sniffed. "Who said anything about butter? I've got a pot of vegetable beef soup simmering over there, so that should appease your boring palate."

Colin strode in, sniffed, and made a beeline to the stove. Raising the lid, he groaned. "You made your vegetable beef soup. Maybe I can cancel my dinner meeting with the Swansons."

He was referring to one of H3's most generous donors, so Arden knew he would never. "Don't worry, there will be plenty of leftovers."

Reaching into a drawer and pulling out a spoon, Colin stole a sample, blowing on it before tasting. He groaned, "So good."

Nick moved to his side, obviously intending to follow Colin's example.

Arden hurried over and smacked his hand. "Not you, too. You can wait for dinner."

As Colin reached for another spoonful, she waved him away.

"Colin, isn't there somewhere you need to be? Maybe preparing for your dinner meeting?"

Dropping the spoon in the sink and raising his hands in surrender, he backed toward the door. "I'm gone."

After he left, Arden turned her attention back to the mixer. "Guess I'll have to go old school and make the bread by hand."

"Can I help? Dr. Weston doesn't need me at the clinic this afternoon, and I've finished my calls to Honduras. Let's do this."

Arden considered his well-defined forearms and, after duly appreciating the sight, decided they would come in handy. She removed the bowl from its position on the mixer and plunked it down on the counter, then retrieved a wooden spoon from the utensil caddy. "How about you do the work, and I supervise?" She crossed to the other side of the island and pulled a barstool up to the counter. "Wash your hands and let's get started."

Nick's deer-in-the-headlights look pleased her to no end. He crossed to the sink and scrubbed in. Literally. As if he were about to perform surgery.

Arden bit back a smile. "While I appreciate your concern for food safety, we don't need a sterile environment. Just come over here and start stirring everything together."

He dried his hands, then picked up the wooden spoon.

Watching him hold it aloft as he contemplated the mess inside the bowl, Arden could picture him in an operating room. Scalpel? Scalpel. Wooden spoon? Wooden spoon.

Nick tentatively moved the ingredients around, raising his eyebrows as it formed a loose dough.

"I'm sensing you don't spend much time in the kitchen." Arden couldn't help but notice the flexing of his forearms as he stirred. By putting him to work, not only did she avoid having to manhandle her way through the stiff ingredients, but she could also admire his muscles.

Still concentrating on the task at hand, he shrugged. "I cook some. Roasting vegetables, making cauliflower rice, stir-fry, that sort of thing. But I've never tried baking. I've always thought it required more skill than I have."

"You've never felt the need for an emergency batch of brownies or chocolate chip cookies?"

He regarded her briefly, cocking an eyebrow.

"No? Me neither." Rolling her eyes, she contradicted her words.

"Do I want to ask how many brownie emergencies you've had? You're certainly comfortable in a kitchen—uncooperative appliances notwithstanding."

"I used to spend more time baking before I got married. Afterward, the closest I came to cooking was discussing dinner party menus." Arden frowned in thought. "My husband wasn't a fan of home cooking, so we ate out unless we were entertaining and then we catered in."

Nick considered her for a moment. "Based on the smell of that soup, I'd say he didn't know what he was missing."

Arden smiled, pleased with his comment. It was nice receiving some praise, even if it was just for a whiff of her soup. Hopefully, he'd feel the same once he tasted it.

She reached across the island and tipped the bowl to look inside. She poked the dough and nodded in satisfaction. "Okay, now we knead."

He looked at her expectantly. "We need what?"

"Dough."

"We have dough."

"I know. Now we knead it."

"Why do we need it if we already have it?"

"Because it forms the gluten." What was so difficult to under-stand? Even non-bakers knew that dough was kneaded before it baked.

Then, like the rising sun over the ocean, understanding dawned on Nick's face.

She laughed. Not a polite chuckle or a socially acceptable ha-

ha. But a full on, doubled-over-hurting belly laugh.

Nick flushed from the base of his neck up to the tips of his ears. "It wasn't that funny," he mumbled.

"Yes. It. Was." Arden choked out her response, then launched back into laughter.

He leaned a hip against the island, crossed his arms and regarded the ceiling until she got herself back under control.

Wiping tears, she said, "Sorry. Don't mean to laugh at you, but all I could think of was that Abbot and Costello routine." With a nostalgic sigh, she added, "That never gets old."

Nick chuckled along. "When you put it that way, it is funny." He turned back to the mixing bowl. "If you're finished LOL-ing, can we get on with this? I think you need to take over. Kneading —with a 'k'—sounds a bit technical."

"I'll show you how. It's not difficult." She moved beside him and reached across for some flour to sprinkle on the granite, her forearm brushing against his chest.

When it tingled, she wondered where her sudden fixation with forearms was coming from. First, she couldn't stop looking at his, and now her own were in sensory overdrive.

She dumped the dough onto the counter and sprinkled it with some of the flour. She patted it into a flat, oblong shape. "First you fold it in half, then you use the heel of your palms to rock it forward. Rotate it a quarter turn and rock it forward again. You keep repeating that for about 10 minutes."

Stepping back, she pointed to the counter. "Now you try."

If she had thought his concentration intense before stirring the ingredients, it shot off the charts now. Tentatively, he touched the dough, gently pressing with his fingers. "Like this?"

"No. Don't be afraid to put some muscle into it. Use the heels of your palms, not your fingers."

This time, he used the correct part of his hand, but he was struggling with the strength of the motion. "Don't be shy. You're forming a gluten network, the structure for the bread.

Your kneading—with a 'k'—must be strong enough to get it going."

After a few more rounds of push pull, the bread was still a sticky glob. Nick pinned her with a look. "See, I told you this was above my pay grade."

"Move, let me in there."

He stepped aside and Arden began working the dough.

Fold, push, turn. Fold, push, turn.

She glanced over. "See? It's all about the rhythm and a firm touch."

She felt his eyes studying her movements. Only the ambient hum of the kitchen appliances interrupted the silence as she continued to manipulate the dough. She could hear her breathing sync with his. The homespun aroma of yeast blended with the unique scent she associated with Nick Monroe. She could get used to having him in her kitchen. Dangerously so.

Clearing her throat, she put some distance between them by retrieving the greased bowl she had set aside. "Now we put the dough in here, cover it with a towel and, over the next hour or so, let the yeast work its magic." Wiping her hands on a towel, she smiled. "Thanks for your help. I can take it from here."

Taking the towel from her to wipe his own hands, he said, "No problem. I enjoyed it. Dinner at the usual time?"

For the first time, Arden realized she would dine with Nick tonight without Colin's presence to provide a buffer. Of course, she knew she would enjoy his company. She had laughed more today than she had in the past five years combined.

However, uneasiness wouldn't be denied its seat at the table. The attraction she felt for him worried her. No, scratch that. It outright scared her. History had shown that she had no talent for relationships, even if she was crazy enough to try again.

But watching him rub stubborn, crusted dough from his hands, she wondered if they could be friends. The camaraderie they shared reminded her of how alone and isolated she had been since her marriage.

Lincoln had made it clear he wanted her to socialize with the wives of those who could advance his career. Once he got her to the altar, Lincoln checked marriage off his list and went on to his next goal, which hadn't included spending time with his wife.

Would it be so wrong for her to enjoy Nick's company while he was in Beacon Bluff? After all, he was heading out of the country soon. What could happen in such a short time? A few laughs, some interesting conversation. What was the harm?

"Before I head out to run some errands, would you like me to take Jonah for a walk?"

At the sound of his name—and his favorite four-letter word—Jonah perked up from where he had claimed a sliver of sunshine for his afternoon nap. He ran to the hook where Arden kept his leash and sat his bum down, hopping up and down with his front legs and barking.

Arden shook her head. "Doesn't seem to matter what I think. You two go on."

She watched them leave, her thoughts wandering to the evening ahead. She hadn't planned on making dessert, but now her mind was trying to think of a healthy-ish idea. Something with fruit. This had nothing to do with impressing Nick, but rather making her guest feel welcome in her home. That's all it was.

LATER THAT AFTERNOON, Nick camped in one of the yet-to-be-renovated rooms upstairs. Arden had graciously allocated this space and a rickety folding table to serve as his makeshift office. Amid a sea of paperwork, his laptop, and several veterinarian supply catalogs, he tried to make sense of what needed to be accomplished.

Nick sighed and rubbed his temples. His focus was slipping, and he knew why. Arden.

Her presence infiltrated his thoughts, even in the midst of important work. He pushed the stray strands of hair off his forehead and attempted to regain his concentration.

Frustration built as he sat before his keyboard, fingers hovering but not pressing any keys. He was attempting to draft an email for the Faith Works selection committee, providing them with ministry-related pictures and a personal bio for the upcoming gala's program. However, the words wouldn't fall into place.

He heard a tap on the door. Nick looked up, and there she was, a concerned expression on her face and Jonah tucked beneath her arm. While an interruption might clear his head, he knew time with Arden would only confuse him more. As much as he wanted to focus on his work and maintain his resolve, her proximity was a magnetic force.

"Hey, Nick," she began. "I hate to bother you, but Jonah's been coughing, and I'm worried it might be related to, you know, the whole near-drowning thing."

She must have finished painting, because her hair was damp, curls slipping free from her hair tie. Bare feet sporting pink toenails peaked from beneath her yoga pants.

Nick frowned. "Coughing? Hand him over, and I'll take a look."

Jonah leaped from her arms into Nick's, squirming with delight and delivering an enthusiastic lick to Nick's cheek.

"He's certainly acting okay." Scooting his chair from the table, Nick laid Jonah across his lap and placed two fingers along the side of his chest. He consulted his watch and was pleased to discover the dog's heart rate was within normal range.

He coaxed Jonah's mouth open and was relieved to see everything pink as it should be, so oxygen levels didn't appear to be compromised.

Keeping Jonah secure with one hand, he used the other to rummage through the papers on the table until he found a stethoscope. He settled the tips into his ears and placed the disc on Jonah's chest. Good. No abnormal sounds coming from the lungs.

He handed Jonah back to Arden who was quick to cuddle the dog beneath her chin. "I don't see or hear anything that concerns me. Has he been in the room with you painting?"

"Yes. I tried keeping him in his crate but all he did was whine. And when that didn't work, he wouldn't stop barking. I know I shouldn't have given in but, well, I did." She stroked Jonah's head and sheepishly grinned.

Nick chuckled. "You're definitely not the first dachshund owner to face their stubbornness head-on. I suspect his cough is related to irritation from the paint fumes. But don't worry too much; he hasn't coughed at all since he's been in here."

Tears welled in her eyes. "I should have known better than to keep him with me."

"This isn't your fault. Your instincts led you to bring him to me. And let's face it, if it weren't for you, we don't know where this little guy would be right now. It's not uncommon for dogs to have sensitive respiratory systems, even without his history," he reassured her. "But just to be safe, keep a close eye on him overnight. If it gets worse or if there are other symptoms, we'll take him in for a chest X-ray."

She nodded. Her fears seemingly put to rest for now, she glanced at his cluttered table. "Sorry I couldn't offer you a proper office. Hopefully you're not too uncomfortable."

"No, not at all." Emotions notwithstanding.

"I have a conference call later regarding the Keeper's Quarters Museum project. What are you working on?"

"Just trying to sort out logistics before I leave for Honduras." His words were meant to remind them both of his short-term status.

She turned toward the door and paused, as if thinking about continuing their conversation.

Remembering the promise he'd made to himself not ten minutes ago about needing distance, Nick chose his words carefully. "Arden, I'm on a time crunch here with this email. Do you mind if we catch up at dinner?"

Her smile faltered, embarrassment flickering across her features. "Of course. I didn't mean to intrude. Thank you for looking at Jonah." She closed the door softly behind herself.

Nick groaned and tipped his head back, looking for absolution from the paint-chipped ceiling. He hated putting that look on her face. Arden's former husband had done a real number on her, he shouldn't be adding to it. But he knew he would cause her more harm in the long run if he encouraged these feelings between them. He was a short timer. Not meant to stick around.

Turning back to his laptop, the words finally flowed more freely. There was no denying the pull he felt toward Arden, even amid organizational challenges and coughing dachshunds demanding his attention. But Honduras needed him, and he was determined to make a difference.

rden put the finishing touches on the dinner table. Assuring herself that she wasn't fussing, she arranged the cloth napkins. The succulent plant arrangement had been hiding in a corner, so why not move it to the table? She was just being hospitable. Practicing for future guests.

She couldn't shake the feeling that Nick had been trying to get rid of her after examining Jonah. Her throat tightened. Lincoln had done likewise—had bestowed upon her brief snippets of time.

Intellectually, she knew Nick was nothing like her former husband. He had shown her nothing but kindness, and he hadn't hesitated to stop work and check on Jonah. But her internal wounds were still sore and slow to heal.

She took a deep breath and pushed those self-defeating thoughts aside. Nick had been honest with her. Yes, he would be leaving soon for Honduras. But that didn't mean they couldn't be friends. They lived under the same roof, after all. He had just been busy earlier, and she had been overly sensitive.

When Nick walked into the kitchen, Arden was standing at

the island slicing fresh tomatoes, mozzarella, and basil for their caprese salad.

Arden noticed his damp hair, pine scent, and closely-shaven face. He had pushed his gray henley sleeves up to the elbows, and the fit across his chest reminded her of his physical fitness.

She was suddenly glad she had changed into a blue peasant-style blouse with a clean pair of jeans. She had left her hair down, pulling it away from her face with a sleek headband.

Jonah had dug a nest in his bed and was now sleeping with just the black tip of nose peeking out from beneath the blanket. No further coughing.

Nick took a seat at the island. "Wow, everything looks and smells fantastic. You didn't need to go to all this trouble."

"No trouble." She loved feeding people and making them comfortable in her home.

Nick reached across and snagged a black olive. "How was the rest of your day? Get much done on the museum project?"

"I did. I contacted my lawyer in Charlotte about finalizing the museum's non-profit status. Trashluggers.com came by and hauled everything out of the lighthouse the museum can't use. Next, I'll attack the place with bleach and a scrub brush."

Nick frowned. "You won't be doing that yourself, will you?"

Her hands stilled as she looked away. The words may have sounded like her former husband, but Arden shoved her disappointment aside. *This is Nick.*

Lincoln had refused to let her do anything herself. He insisted his wife wouldn't dabble in manual labor. He wouldn't even let her cook for the lavish business dinners they hosted. She was sure his pride drove him to insist she hire only the best, but she also suspected he didn't believe she could meet his exacting standards.

Since moving to Beacon Bluff, her confidence had grown. She was still a work-in-progress, but she had learned that Lincoln hadn't been the only one to underestimate her abilities. She had as well. Call it a delinquent bid for rebellion, but she vowed to do as much work herself as possible.

She glanced at Nick, careful to not slice off a finger. "I want to get my hands dirty. Sweat equity, and all that."

He chewed an olive, studying the salad bowl between them. He lifted his head and smiled his understanding. "I get that."

Arden nodded. "I've never had a project all my own. Maybe at some point I'll write a check for someone else to deal with the sore muscles, but for now I'm enjoying the work." She chuckled. "Well, I enjoy the results of the work is what I should say."

"You've never taken on a project before? With your folks' ministry—both in their church and H3—I would imagine you had plenty of opportunities to spearhead a project or two."

Arden's smile faltered, her fingers tightening slightly around the edge of the table.

A beat of silence stretched between them before she turned away, reaching for the salad bowl. "Dinner's ready. Let's eat."

She sat the salad on the table, avoiding eye contact. She felt his gaze follow her to the stove. Arden imagined he realized his comment had pressed on an internal bruise but had no clue as to what it could be.

Still agitated, remembering how useless she had felt within her family and her marriage, Arden wasn't paying close attention to what she was doing. She lifted the bubbling pot of soup and tipped it, pouring the contents into the tureen.

"Ahhhh!" The soup pot had knocked over the tureen. Hot soup spilled across her wrist, causing her to drop the pot back on the stove. She grabbed her wrist and pulled it close to her body.

Through the stinging pain, Arden felt Nick pull her wrist toward himself. When her shirt sleeve stuck to the wound, he gently pulled the fabric away.

"Oh!" She blinked back the tears and bit her lip.

He led her to the sink, thrusting her wrist beneath a flow of cold water. "I know it hurts. Just hold it under the water while I grab the first aid kit from my truck." He dipped his head until she looked him in the eye. "Will you be all right while I'm gone?"

She bit her lip and nodded.

"Okay then. I won't be long."

The pain had started to ease by the time Nick returned.

He sat the medical supplies on the table, then crossed to her side. "Come on, darlin', let's sit over here."

Leading her to a chair, he kneeled before her to inspect the damage. He uncapped a bottle of antiseptic wash and held a dishtowel under her arm as he doused her wrist.

Reaching for some gauze, he warned her, "I'm going to be as gentle as I can, but this may hurt. I need to make sure it's clean."

Arden closed her eyes, took a breath, and nodded. She was determined to remain still and expressionless. Which was all fine and good, but her tear ducts didn't get the memo. One tear escaped, tracking down her cheek. She lifted her free hand to wipe it away, but not before he noticed.

He leaned in close, rested his palm against her cheek, and used his thumb to finish the job.

Arden closed her eyes, leaning into his comforting touch. High voltage comfort.

The back door flew open, banging against the wall and setting Jonah off into a fit of frenzied barking.

"I knew it, Ivey! We got here none too soon, I tell you." Bea charged through the door, Jonah yapping at this new game. "Unhand her, young man."

Nick jerked back his hand, rocked back on his heels, and fell onto his rear end.

Arden jumped up, holding her wrist. "Bea! What are you doing here?"

"Saving the day, it seems. Ivey and I saw your brother heading to dinner with the Swansons, and we figured you and Romeo here needed chaperoning." She sniffed. "And right we were, weren't we, Ivey?"

Ivey stood behind Bea, her understated taupe and cream outfit in stark contrast to Bea's orange and red. She nodded, clutching the bag hanging on her shoulder, yarn overflowing the top.

Nick and Arden just stood there.

Arden wouldn't look at Nick, hoping he'd think her flushed cheeks were from the ladies' abrupt arrival instead of the memory of his hand against her cheek. The tenderness had about been her undoing.

"Well? Is someone going to explain themselves?"

Nick cleared his throat. "Arden burned herself on some hot soup. I was looking after the burn."

Bea studied Arden's face. "Doesn't look like there's any soup on her cheek and that's where you had your hand, mister."

Arden rushed to reply. "Now, Bea, calm down. I was upset and Nick was trying to comfort me." She held out her wrist, displaying the ugly red patch. "See?"

Miss Ivey rushed to Arden's side. "Oh, my dear, that's one angry burn."

"No, really, I'm fine."

Nick cleared his throat. "Ladies, if it's okay with you, I'd like to finish dressing Arden's injury. I'm sure she'll feel more comfortable once I have it bandaged."

Putting her arm around Arden's waist, Miss Ivey said, "Dear, let us take you to the emergency room."

Arden patted her hand. "I believe Nick can take care of this just fine. It's feeling better already."

Bea had remained silent long enough. "He's an animal doctor, and you don't look like no puddy cat to me."

Nick stepped in, taking control of the conversation. "I may not be an M.D., but they covered burns in vet school 101. Miss Ivey, can you find where Arden keeps her cling wrap?" Turning back to Arden, he smiled and asked, "Want to try sitting down again?"

She nodded. "Miss Ivey, I keep it in the drawer next to the stove."

This time around, Nick pulled a chair over and sat in front of her. He applied an antibiotic ointment and covered the burn with non-stick gauze. Smiling his thanks to Miss Ivey, Nick took the cling wrap and covered the bandage.

"There. I'll change the dressing tomorrow, but you're good for tonight. Bea, do you have any ibuprofen in that bag you're carrying?

She found it and sat the bottle on the table. She continued rummaging through the bag and presented an unopened bottle of water with a flourish. "There you go, dear, just what the animal doctor ordered."

Arden swallowed the pills, chasing them with a swig of water. Screwing the cap back on the bottle, she stood, realizing her one-on-one time with Nick wasn't going to happen. Probably just as well. "Ladies, as long as you're here, would you care to join us for dinner?"

Bea grinned. "About time you asked."

NICK WIPED down the counter as Arden ushered Bea and Ivey out the door. Finally. The dynamic duo had drawn out the clean-up process.

He smiled. By cleaning process, he meant them telling him what to do.

After Arden had assured them that Colin was due back any time, Bea gave him one last glare before heading out the door.

Watching through the window as their car pulled away, Arden sighed. "I love them to death, but they can be a handful."

Nick chuckled. "You'll get no argument from me."

He knew without a doubt—he was failing in the biggest way possible at resisting Arden. Every spark of laughter and every effortless conversation chipped away at his resolve. The truth hit him like a weight in his gut: the more he tried to keep his distance, the more impossible she was to resist.

Nick leaned against the countertop, his gaze fixed on the empty kitchen sink. The lines he had drawn were blurring. It was a battle between logic and emotion and, in that moment, emotion was in the lead by a mile.

Arden grabbed the key hanging on a hook near the door and shrugged into an oversized sweater. "While Jonah is sleeping, I need to lock up the lighthouse. Want to come see what it looks like after four dump trucks worked their magic?"

Shrugging into his own jacket, Nick followed her into the lighthouse. She flipped a switch and light revealed the room. The first level looked to be about fifty feet in diameter. There was still a strong odor of must and mildew, but the room was empty. He could see the potential.

"Are you interested in climbing some stairs? It's a clear night and rather mild, so we can climb to the top if you're game."

"Are you sure you don't want to call it a night? Your arm has to be uncomfortable." Part of him wanted her to say goodnight. The stronger, rebellious part of him hoped she'd extend the evening.

She shrugged. "It's fine. The pain reliever seems to have kicked in." She bumped her shoulder against his. "Besides, I had a good doctor."

Nick allowed Arden to precede him up the stairs. He focused on where he set his feet on the narrow stairs, scolding himself for noticing how enticing she was from this vantage point. Some forty steps later, they reached the next level.

As they climbed further, the landings grew smaller, each level narrower in diameter than the one before.

They paused on what he thought was the fifth level. He had lost count.

Arden rested her hands on her knees, panting. "You could at least have the good grace to be out of breath."

"If it makes you feel any better, my quads are screaming."

"Actually, it does." She grinned over her shoulder and resumed climbing the stairs.

Eventually, a metal cage door halted their progress. A large padlock denied them access and an angry looking sign screamed a warning:

*Government Property. Trespassers Will Be Prosecuted.*

"Not exactly subtle, are they?"

"My jurisdiction ends here. The Coast Guard maintains the light itself. If we could go up there, you'd be able to see the full lens apparatus. Truly impressive. The next time they're here, I'll ask them if you can take a look."

Nick didn't want to ruin the moment by reminding her that unless the Coast Guard showed up soon, he'd be gone.

He helped her yank on the black metal door, and they stepped into the night. Nick stopped, unprepared for the world spread below. Dumbstruck, he absorbed the darkness, soaking in the view softened by the moon's glow.

The only sound was muffled waves lapping onto shore. They stood on the narrow iron walkway that hugged the perimeter. The beam flashed bright above their heads, then waned as it made its circuit.

Arden, too, seemed reluctant to interrupt the silence. Leaning her good arm against the iron railing, she tipped her face to the sky. The light breeze blew back loose tendrils of hair so he could take full advantage of the moonlight softening her profile. Her eyes were closed.

He looked his fill without her knowing.

Nick knew she had no idea how lovely she was. If she did, she wouldn't seem so ill-at-ease in her own skin. Her cheekbones provided a resting place for her thick lashes. It was easy to imagine her ocean-colored eyes, full of intelligence and insight.

Her nose was perfect for her face, narrow with a slightly upturned tip. And her lips...

Well, he'd better stop, or his mind would wander where it shouldn't. Like the sign said—no trespassing.

Coming to life, she sat down, legs dangling from the gallery. Glancing over at him, she said, "Join me?"

ARDEN BRACED herself as Nick settled beside her, his shoulder brushing hers. Bringing him up here had been pure impulse. This was her haven, the place where she escaped the world and all its complications. She often sought its solace, even during the day. But at night, when the lighthouse came alive with light, piercing the surrounding darkness, it was nothing short of magic.

And she wanted to share that magic with Nick.

Nick leaned back on his hands, staring up at the sky. "What do you think of when you come out here at night?"

Arden noticed that the earlier cloud cover had made way for a blanket of stars. "I see distance."

He frowned. "Distance? I'm not sure what you mean."

She scooted forward until her arms rested against the lower railing, her chin propped on her hands. She took her time answering, weighing whether she was ready to share something so personal. But there was something about him—something that made her trust that her thoughts and feelings would be safe.

"When Mom and Dad left me in Charlotte, some well-meaning soul assured me I only had to look to the stars for comfort. That somewhere in Honduras, they too were looking at the very same stars, missing me as well."

"That's a beautiful sentiment."

She snorted. "It's ridiculous."

Her throat constricted with remembered pain. "All I saw was the vast amount of space that stood between us. Those stars that were supposed to comfort a seventeen-year-old girl only empha-sized my loneliness. I was told they were points of light leading the way to my family. All I saw were balls of burning sulfur standing in our way."

*Yikes.* She hadn't meant to go that far. Reveal quite so much.

Nick let the silence hang in the night air and she stifled the urge to squirm. Had she shared too much? What must he think of her? Her parents had left to do God's work. Who was she to resent that?

"I can't imagine how you must have felt. Such a tough age for a girl to lose her mom."

Arden turned her head and saw an utter lack of judgment on his face. She ignored the stinging behind her eyes, refusing to revisit the feelings of that confused teenage girl.

"Thank you. You're the only person I admitted that to." She laughed, trying to lighten the mood. "Not sure why."

He shrugged. "I'm safe. You know I won't be around long. Plus the darkness, this whole atmosphere, invites confidences."

"Then what about you? Your turn to spill your guts."

He laughed. "No guts to spill. But I can empathize with the price of ministry. My dad was an itinerant preacher, and his calling took a toll on me and my mom."

Happy to turn the spotlight elsewhere, Arden asked, "In what way?"

"It was kind of like being a military kid. Moving from place to place, never knowing how long you'd stay put. Didn't give us much time to establish relationships and, as time went by, I decided why bother? We'd just be leaving, anyway."

Arden's heart ached for little boy Nick. "What about your mom?"

Nick looked out to the horizon, where the ocean blended into the night sky. "Mom is a nester." He bumped her shoulder. "Much like you."

"Me? You see me as a nester?" Warmth spread across her chest, pleased with his insight.

"Absolutely. You're building a nest here at Keeper's Quarters for others to nestle into. You love feeding people and creating beautiful spaces."

Arden had never felt so seen in her life.

He sat up, joining her at the rail. "Unfortunately, Mom didn't have anywhere to build a nest to call her own. Most of the churches allowed her to re-vamp their parsonages, within reason. But it seemed just when she got them the way she liked, Dad got the call to move on. I always felt so bad for her. All her efforts being left behind for the next family to enjoy."

At least Arden was a teenager when her parents left. His dad's ministry had impacted Nick throughout his formative years. No wonder he had a hard time staying in one place.

Arden tilted her head to get a better look at his face. The shadows hinted at his defined cheekbones and full lips. "So, I coped by shaking my fist at the stars. How about you?"

A wide grin stretched across his face. "I got a Golden Retriever."

The breeze caught her laugh, giving it wings. "Of course you did."

"Christy was my lifeline, the one friend I could take with me from place to place. Don't know what I'd have done without her." He winked with a wicked grin. "She commiserated with many an adolescent crush over the years."

His attention turned back to the murky horizon and his voice grew thoughtful. "When she was diagnosed with cancer, I was sure the world was ending. We could only afford the bargain vet clinics, and I knew my folks couldn't swing any expensive treatment. But there was a vet in our congregation who offered a second opinion at no charge. Ends up Christy had a tick-borne disease and not lymphoma."

Her heart tripped with relief. "You got a happy ending."

"I sure did. She lived long enough to see me off to college. And now you know one reason why I became a vet. I wanted to provide happy endings for other families."

Nick reached out and touched her elbow, encouraging her to scoot back so they were leaning against the lighthouse, legs stretched out before them. "What about you? Did you ever get your happy ending?"

This time she couldn't keep herself from squirming. He broached a tricky subject, one she wasn't sure she wanted to address. "Let's just say I thought I did, but it didn't work out."

"Your husband?"

She sighed. "Yes."

When she didn't continue, he prompted, "And it didn't work out?"

"You could say that." She stared across the darkened ocean, refusing to look his way. "I am a widow after all."

"Were you two happy before he passed?"

She could tell he suspected the truth, but wanted it spelled out.

He angled his body toward her, amping up the impact of his masculinity. His warmth reached out, inviting her to sink into it as if it were laundry fresh from the dryer.

She wasn't sure if it was the lure of that warmth or the genuine interest radiating from his face, but she wanted to let down her guard. Give up the fight.

Finally turning toward him, she said, "I'm not sure why you want to hear all this...but, no, I wasn't particularly happy. In fact, looking back, I now realize how miserable I was."

His silence was patient, so she continued.

"His family were leaders in my dad's church, and our families were close. It seemed natural that I would stay with them while I finished my last year of high school.

"Lincoln was several years older and quite the ladies' man. You know, the Big-Man-on-Campus type. He always seemed beyond my reach. But when he came home from college that year, he paid attention to me. Once I graduated, he pursued me like crazy."

Nick raked his hair back from his forehead. "I'm sure you appreciated his attention."

"Yep. In fact, I appreciated it all the way down the aisle." She tried to keep the bitter taste from flavoring her words, but it was a useless effort.

Nick groaned and put his arm around her, pulling her against his side. "From your tone, I'm assuming that was a bad thing."

Arden rested her head on his shoulder, lost in her memories. "I came to realize that Lincoln was only interested in me because of my family. Charlotte is a hub of the Bible belt, and Dad's church became one of the first mega-churches. Always on the lookout for an edge, Lincoln decided I could enhance his status because, after all, John Bennett would only allow his daughter to marry an upstanding, God-fearing citizen."

Nick sat perfectly still, allowing her to gather her thoughts.

"I won't rehash my entire marriage, so I'll skip straight to the end. The night he rolled over that guardrail? It was two a.m. and he was leaving his girlfriend's condo. Need I say more?"

He pulled her closer, placing both arms around her.

She hesitated before resting against his chest.

"I'm so sorry."

She shrugged, her voice small. "Not your fault."

"No, but I can still hate that it happened to you." He tightened his hold around her shoulders. "In case you didn't know, he was a real jerk."

She giggled. "You think?"

Nick added his own quiet laughter, and she loved the vibration beneath her cheek.

She smiled, burying her nose into his shirt. The warm male scent woke the swarm of butterflies inside her stomach.

He drew back and tipped her chin so he could see her face.

His gaze roamed her features, as if he were memorizing each detail.

She saw flickers of emotion in his eyes, like an old-fashioned movie reel. Empathy moved out, surprise moved in. Confusion followed, being chased by acceptance.

The tip of his index finger traced along her nose, wandering onto her cheek. "Do you remember those dot-to-dot puzzles we did as kids?"

Too nervous to speak, she nodded.

"If I trace your freckles, what picture do you think I'd find?"

She swallowed. "You tell me."

Instead, he replaced his finger with his lips.

It was as if the butterflies had escaped and were now brushing across her cheek. She closed her eyes and held her breath, not wanting to frighten them away. She knew he wouldn't be in town long. She also knew that at this moment, she didn't care.

He must have felt the same, because he barely whispered, "Arden," just before his lips found hers.

Breathing stopped. Lips tingled. Shooting stars flashed behind her eyelids.

Nick made a delicious sound in the back of his throat, the timber strumming a chord buried within. His lips lightly moved across hers yet demanded a response.

She tasted the hint of the chocolate dipped strawberries they had eaten—sweet and decadent, much like the man whose lips were nibbling hers as if they were his dessert of choice.

The hand at her waist clenched, as if fighting the urge to pull her even closer. Propriety dictated he win the battle, but the woman of her prayed he wouldn't.

She struggled to breathe, having a new appreciation for how Jonah must have felt.

His accelerated heartbeat thudded against her palm, a silent confirmation that he, too, felt the weight of this newfound intimacy.

She meant to push him away, to create distance, but instead, her traitorous fingertips traced the contours of his muscles.

She had no idea how long they sat like that—lips joined, fingers exploring.

Finally, he lifted his head, but he didn't go far. His thumb brushed her cheek. His eyelids were heavy as he licked his lips. Good thing they were seated. That look alone had the power to cut her legs out from underneath her.

"I know an apology is in order, but you won't be getting one." His voice sounded as if gravel lined his throat.

Somewhere, from beneath the heavy haze of longing, Arden discovered enough strength to push away and scramble to her feet. Her knees trembled, but they held firm.

Five years of marriage...and never had a kiss left her this breathless, unraveling every last defense. This was not good.

Gripping her arms around her waist, she said, "I'm sure Colin must be home by now. We should head back downstairs."

Nick nodded, his gaze steady on her face, though she couldn't bring herself to meet his eyes. But she knew what she would see —disappointment.

But he said nothing as he rose with effortless grace and reached around her to open the heavy door. "After you."

Arden began the downward trek, forcing herself to walk and not rush. She couldn't wait to reach the solitude of her room. She had revealed much of herself tonight, given so much. It was time to gather Jonah close, crawl into bed, and dive back undercover.

# CHAPTER 11

$\mathcal{M}$aybe he should have a tech take an X-ray of his brain during his next shift at the clinic. Obviously, he had a screw rattling around in there.

Nick moved the stepladder to the next section of drywall that required his attention. It was the morning after the heart-to-heart with Arden that led to that spine-tingling, eye-opening kiss. A kiss that should never have happened.

Jonah trotted into the room, sniffing along the hardwood floors, leaving a trail of damp nose prints in the drywall dust. He found a paint-splattered drop cloth wadded in a corner and began his pre-nap ritual of circling and pawing the cloth. A hearty groan signaled his satisfaction as he settled into a mid-morning nap.

"So, boy, where's your mom?" Nick looked over his shoulder as he climbed the ladder. "Not that I'm looking for her. In fact, I'd just as soon not run into her. Not until I get my mind right."

He reached above his head for the next patch of abused drywall. Spackling required little brain power, so he continued his conversation with his slumbering companion.

"What would you do if you had kissed a woman who was so far off limits, she should be wrapped in yellow caution tape?

Jonah snored, oblivious to Nick's angst.

"You should have been there, buddy." He rested his arms against the top of the ladder and gazed out a window. "It was like a scene out of some old movie. Breeze in her hair, the world at our feet. And her vulnerability. With everything she's been through? I had no choice. I'm not made of stone, you know."

Even with Vanessa—who he had been convinced was the love of his life—he had never felt as if he were caught in the tractor beam of some alien spaceship. Just remembering Arden in his arms, his chest tightened and his breathing quickened. As a vet, he knew hyperventilation could signal several physical ailments. But as a man, he knew the truth. He was falling for Arden Gray.

The aliens were winning.

Nick descended the ladder and shoved it to the next section. So now what? Well, for one thing, he could not let this go any further. Vanessa may not have turned out to be his one and done, but she had reinforced a valuable lesson he had already learned from his parents—marriage and ministry didn't mix.

Speaking of ministry, Arden was adamant that she was meant to stay in Beacon Bluff. God had called them to different parts of the globe, and there was no getting around that.

What about his promise to Colin about not hurting his sister? Nick wasn't the only one developing feelings. Arden's sweet response to his kiss had assured him of that. The last thing he wanted was to fly off to Honduras, proving yet again that a man couldn't be trusted with her heart.

Despite being convinced that backing away was the thing to do, he felt an actual ache around his heart. Arden was kind, funny, and she seemed to get him. He *liked* her. When he was with her, he wasn't the ministry guy, only focused on his goals. When he wasn't with her, he wished he were.

The loneliness that dogged him since being shuffled from

parsonage to parsonage didn't exist when they were together. With her, he felt complete. If he were to ever fall in love and marry, he couldn't picture a better candidate.

Even so, he had commitments to keep. He had signed a contract with H3.

Nick climbed down the ladder and gathered Jonah into his arms. "What do you say, buddy? Any ideas on how I keep up my end of the bargain and help her around this place without getting in over my head?"

The dog tilted his head, giving Nick a look that only confirmed his own thoughts—Nick may as well have had green skin, an oversized head, and big black eyes.

Two days may have passed since The Kiss, but Arden had still had tossed through restless night. She climbed out of her SUV, grabbed Jonah from the back seat, and headed up the steps to Miss Ivey's stucco bungalow. The Dresden blue shutters and prolific camellia bushes with their winter coral blooms reflected Miss Ivey's genteel sensibilities.

Bea's 1980s wood-paneled Ford Bronco sat in the crushed oyster shell driveway, warning Arden this wouldn't be a quick in and out.

She had left Nick at the house, repairing the upstairs drywall. At least, that's what it sounded like he was doing. Arden hadn't ventured upstairs to confirm or deny her assumption. The last thing she wanted was to interact with him until she gained control of her unruly thoughts.

Before pressing the doorbell, she sat in a blue rocker, settling Jonah on her lap. Only the creaking of her chair as she set it into motion interrupted the peacefulness of the quaint neighborhood street.

"Jonah, what are we to do? Nick's getting under my skin."

Her sweet friend had his chin resting on his outstretched paws, and his warm brown eyes looked up at her with a surprising amount of sympathy.

Maybe she should come back another time to pick up the blankets Miss Ivey had knitted for the guest rooms. A time when her brain wasn't twisting in the aftermath of Nick's kiss. Assuming there would be a time when last night's memories didn't crowd out every other thought.

She'd kissed Nick Monroe, and she had liked it. A lot.

So where did that leave them? Why had he kissed her? Did he enjoy the experience, or had she disappointed him? Did he regret it? Did he want to do it again?

As for her feelings on the matter, she wanted to wrap that evening around her and wallow in it for days. She also wished it had never happened. How could two such contradictory emotions live within the same brain?

On the one hand, if she closed her eyes, she could still feel Nick's strength surround her. Her nose tingled with the memory of his woodsy pine scent and the feel of his lips tracing her freckles. She felt the steady pulse of his heartbeat beneath her cheek.

As for her lips, well, they warmed from the memory. If she were looking to add a man to her life—which she wasn't—someone like him would check all the boxes.

But that was just it. It couldn't be him. Every instinct screamed not to become involved with a man who, not only was called to an international mission field, but was also involved with her family's ministry. The same one that took her parents away from her when all she had wanted was for them to stay.

Of course, she had no space for a relationship at this juncture in her life. She was just now emerging from the box Lincoln had sealed her into. Keeper's Quarters was more than an idea scratched on some scrap paper and it was so close to becoming a reality. One that proved that Arden Gray was more than Lila and John's daughter or Lincoln's accessory.

Arden looked to the side as the front door opened.

Bea was standing in the doorway with hands on her hips. "Girl, what are you doing out here by yourself? Come on inside before you rock yourself into next week."

Arden hadn't realized she'd been pumping the rocker as if she were running the Kentucky Derby.

Jonah jumped from her lap and pushed between Bea's ankles, waltzing into Miss Ivey's as if he owned the place.

She followed her dog through the door. "Of course. I just took a moment to catch my breath before ringing the doorbell."

Bea raised an eyebrow, but she let Arden's lame explanation float on by.

Miss Ivey bustled out of the kitchen and put an arm around Arden's shoulders. "Come right on in, dear. Join us in the back and you can sit a spell before you leave." She led Arden back to the kitchen, where a platter of snickerdoodles and a pitcher of iced sweet tea sat at the ready.

Bea had made a detour into the sitting room and entered the kitchen loaded down with six knitted blankets, each a solid shade of blue, green, or beige. Perfect hues for a beach-side bed and breakfast. Miss Ivey had outdone herself with the beautiful and intricate wave pattern.

Bea set the stack on a nearby bench and pulled up a chair.

Miss Ivey poured sweet tea and pushed the cookies toward Arden.

Jonah hopped up on the bench and burrowed between the layers of blankets, his entire body buried except for his fluffy, reddish-brown tail that hung down the side of the pile.

"I don't mean to take up your time, ladies. I'm sure you have things to do." Arden reached for a cookie and took a bite.

Reaching across the table, Miss Ivey touched her hand. "You know we're here for you if you need to talk about anything."

A snort came across the table. Bea added, "We may be old, but that gives us a whole lot of experience to draw on. Maybe we can help."

Arden regarded these two dear women, and it was as if the warm comfort of one of Miss Ivey's blankets filled her insides. Whether they meant to, they had become her *de facto* mothers since she arrived in Beacon Bluff.

Maybe she should talk about these ridiculous feelings. She wouldn't talk about the kiss—that would just be weird. But maybe if she shared her confusion with these two dear souls who loved her, they would help her make sense of it all.

Where to begin?

"I find the best place to start is at the beginning." Reading her mind as any good *de facto* mother would, Bea settled back, honing her focus on Arden.

Miss Ivey picked up her ever-present knitting and the soothing click-click of her needles began. "It's about that handsome vet, of course."

Arden bristled. "What do you mean, 'of course'?"

Ivey looked up and paused her knitting. "Like Bea said, we've been around the block ourselves a time or two. We can sniff out romance a mile away. Especially when it involves someone we care about."

Sighing, Arden relaxed. "It's not a romance. At least, I don't think it is."

"But you want it to be?" Bea's question was a punch to the gut.

"No! Yes. Maybe?"

As if choreographed, they each gave her a long look and a raised eyebrow.

"I'm not in the market for romance. As you know, Lincoln made it quite clear I'm not good at that sort of thing. And even if I ignored that painful experience, I can't compete with Honduras."

She swallowed her feelings before they could spill out. "If I lost that battle with my own parents, what makes me think I could ever win with Nick?"

Ivey discarded her knitting with surprising vengeance. She took both of Arden's hands and squeezed them with purpose. "You listen here, darlin'. Those things you mentioned, none were of your doing. That no-good husband of yours didn't treat you right. That's his failing, not yours. He's the one who violated God-honoring marriage vows. You can see that, can't you?"

Arden tightened her lips and looked away.

Bea took her turn. "As for your parents, they're good people doing their best to serve God. I can't say as I could have done what they did—leaving you to fend for yourself. But knowing them, I am sure they did the best they could at the time and meant you no harm. Maybe you need a heart-to-heart with them. You know, clear the air and come to an understanding so you can move forward. If not with Nick, then with someone else."

Arden shrugged, raking her hands through her hair, pushing the curls back from her face. "I hear what you're saying and even believe it on some level. But deep down—the level that counts—it still hurts."

Bea lifted a brow. "You need to work on that."

"I'm not sure how."

"Maybe start by opening your heart a bit to Nick?"

Just hearing Bea's words chased the breath from her lungs and squeezed her heart. She had begun to find her way here in Beacon Bluff, separate from a husband or her family. She wasn't sure she could trust herself to stand firm if she made the mistake of falling in love with Nick.

*Hold your horses, girl. Who said anything about the "L" word?*

Her panic must have spread across her face, because Bea said, "I'm not sayin' you should hand over your heart on some fancy platter, but would it be so terrible to just have some fun with a friend?"

"I don't know. It might be."

"Baby girl, what's important is that you don't let your past experiences get in the way of what God may have for you. It's His job to guide your steps, and yours is to follow without throwing obstacles in front of yourself. I have no idea what's meant for you and that young man. But what if you're allowing your fear to get in the way of God's purpose? Is that something you want to risk?"

Arden let Bea's words settle, their weight pressing against the walls she'd built around her heart. Was she really protecting herself? Or just letting fear dictate her future? The thought unsettled her more than she cared to admit.

Arden stood, hugged her friends, wiped her cheeks, and called to Jonah.

He poked his nose out from his den of blankets, then jumped down and shook himself awake. The motion started at the tip of his nose and worked its way down his long body, stopping shy of his tail. He sat down and sniffed the air, ready for all the snacks.

Arden smiled. Nothing got by that nose—especially snicker-doodle cinnamon.

The three women laughed at his antics, and then Miss Ivey snapped her fingers. "Wait! You can't leave yet. I have something for Jonah."

She scurried out of the kitchen and returned a few moments later with a multi-colored wad of yarn in her hands. She kneeled next to the dog, her back shielding him from Arden's view. When Miss Ivey stood, there sat Jonah in a custom made, hand-knit green and yellow argyle sweater. Complete with a matching hat tied beneath his chin.

Arden choked on a laugh. "Miss Ivey, you shouldn't have." She *really* shouldn't have.

Jonah pranced to the door and paused to look over his shoulder as if to say, "Coming?"

Arden grabbed the pile of blankets. Time to go back home, even if it meant seeing Nick again.

# CHAPTER 12

The noise—the barking, the whining, the blow drying, and so much more.

It had been five days since her and Nick's kiss. Five days of barely seeing him, despite sharing the same living space. The time for avoidance was over, however, since today was the day for them to emcee the charity dog show.

Arden observed the large room—some sort of soundstage for Carolina News Now. The metal building absorbed little sound, so every woof reverberated.

Volunteer staff ran from crate to crate, checking on the furry stars of the show.

She clutched Jonah tighter, ensuring he didn't take part in the mayhem.

Tiffany caught her eye from across the room and headed toward her, dodging a poodle mix streaking across her path and a golden lab pulling its handler in hot pursuit. Today, the reporter was dressed much more casually than she had been for the on-camera beach interview.

Arden heaved a huge inward sigh of relief. Her own jeans and sweater matched the occasion.

"Hi, Arden. Is Nick with you?"

"Yes, he's parking the truck."

"Here he is now. Good to see you, Nick." Tiffany smiled.

Nick put his arm around Arden, and she was sucked right back into the vortex from their night under the stars. If she closed her eyes, she could imagine they were still there. Isolated at the top of the world. Indulging in a moment that had no place between them.

Still, she hadn't forgotten her conversation with Bea and Miss Ivey about not being so guarded. Arden willed herself to relax. Not quite leaning against him, but not stiff as a body board either.

Nick smiled. "Glad to be here."

Arden remembered to breathe again once Nick dropped his arm and reached for Jonah, who was turning himself inside out to get to Nick.

Tiffany glanced at the clipboard in her hand. "Let me go over how the day is set up. What you see here is the staging area. The dog show will take place next door, with games and inflatables nearby. Families can interact with their new best friends in designated secure locations." Tiffany dropped her voice as if she imparted top secret information. "Happy parents have trouble saying no to kids and adorable dogs. Know what I'm saying? Come on, I'll take you next door. That's where the judging table is set up."

Arden and Nick followed her into an adjoining sound stage. This one had artificial turf instead of concrete, and a low, picketed fence "yard" was in the middle, with several rows of spectator seats rising along the sides. A table with two chairs was in the center.

Circling the arena was a castle bouncy house, Skee-Ball, arcade games, and stations for kid-friendly crafts. Food vendors were setting up and Arden's stomach rumbled its request for a deep-fried Oreo. Craft artisans displayed their wares—dog bandanas, handmade dog toys, and home-baked dog treats, to name a few.

It warmed Arden's heart to see how many caring people had come together to pull this off. She prayed many lonely pups would find their forever families. She would do her absolute best to help make it happen—no matter how out of place she might feel.

After glancing at her watch, Tiffany said, "The doors are about to open. You have about half an hour before you'll be needed at the judges' table. Feel free to walk around in the meantime."

The last was said over her shoulder as a volunteer came and told her an electrical circuit blew and a bevy of wet dogs needed a blow-out.

Once the doors opened to the public, it wasn't long before a circle of admirers gathered around Jonah.

Sensing he was the dog of the hour, his tiny body vibrated with energy, his eyes bright and his nose working overtime, sniffing the proffered hands before giving them a lick. From the comfort of Arden's arms, he held court, gracing his subjects with his presence.

"Dr. Monroe, Jonah is so thin. Is he really okay?" A young girl around twelve years of age gently petted Jonah's head, a concerned furrow on her face.

"He's actually gained weight since Ms. Gray took him in." Nick placed his arm across Arden's shoulder and gave her an incandescent smile. "Who knows how long he wandered around fending for himself before his guardian angel took him in."

Arden's heart hopped, skipped, and jumped. That smile should be registered with the FBI.

"Does he do any tricks?" A young boy tugged at her sleeve. She bent down and brought Jonah to the boy's eye level.

"Not unless you count playing hide and seek when it comes time for a bath. Once I found him inside a kitchen cabinet."

The little boy giggled, shot his mom a look, then whispered, "I don't like baths either." Then he took off toward the ice cream cart, his mom in hot pursuit.

Arden made to stand, but Jonah chose that moment to bark at a passing balloon vendor with his floating missiles of death. She tipped sideways, but Nick caught her elbow and brought her to her feet.

His lips came wickedly close to her ear. "Steady there, Blondie."

Her smile felt as if it were molded from plastic, such was the effort not to react to his mint-laced breath caressing her skin.

Fortunately, the surrounding crowd threw out more questions, so the moment passed.

Nick and Arden continued to interact with the crowd, and the three of them posed for countless selfies. When Jonah couldn't stop squirming, she and Nick excused themselves and went outside so the dog could take care of business.

Arden inhaled slowly through her nose, exhaling through her mouth. Wasn't that supposed to alleviate anxiety? Bea's advice about being open only upped her anxiety.

They both focused on Jonah picking his potty spot with far more attention than it warranted. The awkward silence between them had her wiping sweaty palms against her jeans. What was going on? They'd never lacked for conversation before. The only thing that had changed between them had been The Kiss. He must regret it.

Out of the corner of her eye, she noticed Nick licking his lips then applying lip balm. Jumping in to fill the conversational void, she asked, "What flavor is that? My favorite is strawberry."

The second the words left her mouth, even before Nick's disconcerted frown, Arden prayed for the superpower of rewinding time. Why was she bringing his lips into the conversation?

"Uh...mint." His cheeks were the color of discomfort and, after a quick look at her lips, his gaze darted somewhere over her head.

Was he imagining a strawberry-mint lip mash-up, or was it just her?

Tiffany saved the moment by sticking her head out the side door and motioning them inside. "We're ready for you."

They both took off after her, as if judging a dog show could save the free world.

Once they reached their table, Arden lifted Jonah onto the surface to sit between them. She reached into her bag, then snapped a jaunty blue and green plaid bow tie around his neck.

She caught the look Nick threw her way.

"What? He's dressing for success. It could be worse, you know. He could have worn the coat of many colors Miss Ivey knitted for him, with the matching hat."

The background music stopped, and Carolina News Now's beloved chief meteorologist welcomed everyone to the show and warmed up the crowd with cheesy dog jokes.

"What did one flea say to the other?"

The crowd yelled in unison. "What did he say?"

"Should we walk or take the dog?"

He had the crowd howling with laughter, even Nick and Arden.

Jonah bounced between them, eager to join in on the joke.

Once the laughter receded, the emcee said, "Seriously, we are here to benefit a wonderful cause. Area shelters and rescues are still overcrowded in the aftermath of Hurricane Camilla. We won't rest until every dog has found their 'furever' family!

"Let's welcome our very own celebrity couple, Arden Gray and Dr. Nick Monroe, with their rescued miniature dachshund, Jonah!

"Our first category is Best Wiggle Tush."

~

AS A VETERINARIAN, adorable animals were his stock-in-trade. But as he watched the incoming parade of dogs—most of whom were the offspring of mix-and-match breeds—Nick was as charmed as the little boy who didn't like baths.

Even Jonah stood to get a better view of the contestants.

Arden grinned and looked over her shoulder as they made their way to the center of the ring.

Nick chuckled. "This sure beats repairing drywall."

He watched as her smile disappeared.

A production assistant approached with a lapel mic and attached it to Arden's shirt before doing the same for him.

As the assistant hustled away to her next task, Nick grabbed Arden's hand, knowing the action would play well for the audience. But he also wanted to reassure her.

The mics weren't live yet, so he said, "Forget you have that thing on. You'll be great."

She looked at him. He didn't know what she was searching for on his face, but apparently, she found it. Nodding, she turned to the crowd.

Nick was relieved they had moved on from Jonah's potty break. Cute animals could fill any awkward space. But how was he supposed to keep his distance when she talked about lips? He had the sudden urge to go out and buy some strawberry lip balm.

Since they got the signal that the microphones were live, Nick decided to play with the crowd. "I don't know, Arden. I'm not sure we'll see any noteworthy wiggles from this group."

As anticipated, he drew a round of boos.

Arden's gasp was heard around the room. "How can you say that? There's not a bad wiggle in the bunch!"

He shrugged. "I'm not convinced."

Arden directed her attention to the grinning handlers and the half-dozen dogs in front of her. She thrust Jonah's leash into Nick's hand, plopped on the floor and motioned for the first dog,

Spike, who seemed to be the product of a love match between a corgi and a basset hound.

Where had the camera-shy Arden gone?

"Come here, fella. Come see Aunt Arden." Her baby talk was music to Spike's ears.

He lumbered over, climbed into her lap, and wiggled for all he was worth as he kissed her face.

Maybe it was the strawberry lip balm.

Whatever it was, the crowd went wild.

She continued whipping the rest of the contestants into a frenzy of wiggles, then returned them to their handlers to deal with the aftermath.

He had to hold Jonah, since he added his growls to the mix. Apparently, the pup wasn't crazy about his mom paying so much attention to other dogs.

After awarding Spike the Best Wiggle Tush ribbon, they continued on to judge the Best Couch Potato, Best Conversationalist, Best Senior Dog, and Best Kisser categories.

Speaking of best kissers...

This would not do. He wiped a hand over his face.

He looked over, to find Arden kneeling so Jonah could lick the cotton candy residue off a little girl's cheek.

Both Arden and the little girl were giggling. She would make a great mom.

*Whoa. Put the brakes on there, buddy.*

Perhaps he should rethink this #Arick thing. He couldn't afford to keep losing focus. He was so close to getting on a plane to Honduras. He was so close to performing the work God had called him to, at the place He called him to do it.

At the least, deepening his feelings for Arden would distract him and slow his progress. At the worst, his heart could be broken. Maybe even Arden's. He needed to stick to his guns and somehow insert a friendly distance between them.

His dark thoughts were interrupted by a man approaching

him and reaching across the picket fence to shake his hand. "Nick Monroe?"

"Yes. What can I help you with?

"I wanted to take this opportunity to say hello and introduce myself. I'm Cal Porter with Faith Works."

Nick straightened his shoulders, all thoughts abandoned in favor of focusing on the man before him.

Cal Porter was of medium height, medium build, and had medium brown hair. But his wide smile distinguished him as bright and personable.

"Such a pleasure to meet you. What brings you to the area?"

"I was meeting with Colin Bennett, finalizing the details for the upcoming Faith Works gala. He mentioned you were here judging a rescue dog show, and I just had to stop by. I must say, I didn't expect to be so entertained, but you and Ms. Gray know how to work a crowd."

"It was nothing, really. We were just having fun while helping a cause we both believe in."

"Maybe so. But I'm glad you're immersing yourself in the community. That's important to the Faith Works grant selection process."

At that point, Arden and Jonah joined them.

Jonah made it clear he wanted Nick to hold him so he could more closely inspect this new person.

Arden handed him over.

Cal Porter held out his hand to Arden. "Ms. Gray, what a pleasure to meet you. You're John and Lila's daughter, is that right?"

Nick watched her happy glow dim. "Yes. And Colin is my brother."

"I can't express how pleased I am that H3 has partnered with Faith Works for this year's gala." He paused, casting his gaze between them. "Are you two an item? I can't say I'd be sorry if you were. Many a ministry has benefited from the Bennett family's assistance."

Arden's cheeks pinkened, and she glanced away.

Nick reached for her hand, pulling her attention back to the conversation. "We've become close."

A side glance showed him that Arden managed a smile, weak though it was. "H3 is my parents' and brother's ministry. As much as I love the people of Honduras, I can't claim that connection."

Nick wasn't sure why she felt the need to set the record straight. Cal obviously was impressed with her family's work and his connection to them. Couldn't she let it be? It's not like he outright lied. They had gotten close. That was her end of the deal, right? Help him look good before the grant committee?

"Well, I need to be off now. I just wanted to introduce myself and say hello. It's a long way back to Atlanta, so I'd better get started." Cal nodded to Nick. "You'll be hearing from someone soon to set up your on-site interview with the committee. Take care."

"Thank you." He watched the man walk away, hornets buzzing in his stomach. The grant competition was even more real for having met Cal Porter.

#Arick was working. No turning back now.

# CHAPTER 13

The next afternoon, Nick found Arden in the kitchen with seashells and all sorts of earthy material spread across the table. Her hair was perched on top of her head, just waiting for a stiff wind to break it loose. Even with no makeup, and a stretched out white t-shirt sporting splatters of crafts past, she was a sight for sore eyes. One bare foot reached over to rub across the other as she considered the items before her and bit her lip.

He swallowed a groan. His own lip buzzed at the memory of how hers had felt beneath his. What was it about this woman that drew him? He had prayed for God to take this desire away, certain that it could only lead to heartache.

The call from Don Carlos yesterday had interrupted him before he could make another mistake.

Clearing his throat, he walked up to the table and motioned to what she was working with. "What's all this?"

Arden jumped at the sound of his voice, a delightful blush spreading across her cheeks. "I'm making wreaths for the double-front doors. Something that says, 'Hi, come on in. Awesomeness awaits.'"

He picked up some greenish moss, rubbing it between his fingers. "You're asking for a lot from twigs and seashells, aren't you?"

"Not at all." She shrugged. "You're a man, so I don't expect you to get it."

Her statement hung in the air between them. Yes, he was certainly a man. A man with an inconvenient interest in the woman standing before him.

"Then I won't offer to help. But do you think you could take a break? I'm sure Jonah wants to take a walk along the beach."

The words "walk" and "beach" had Jonah barking and skidding into the back door. He shook his head at the impact.

Arden shrugged. "Hardwood floors and dachshunds don't mix." Turning her attention back to Nick, she frowned. "You did that on purpose. You know he won't give me any peace until he gets his w-a-l-k."

Nick was unrepentant. "Guilty."

Of course, he wasn't convinced of the wisdom of seeking her out, but Nick respected her opinion, and he needed a neutral perspective on a dilemma he was facing with Vets Without Boundaries. Someone who knew the area and the particular challenges that ministries faced.

In addition, he had to tell her about the decision he'd come to.

Jonah pulled them along the path to the beach, as if he were the one taking them on a walk. As always, he stuck to the loose sand, not venturing close to the water.

Arden tipped her chin toward the dog. "Do you think he'll ever overcome his fear of the water?"

Just as the words left her mouth, Jonah sat down and refused to budge. He paid maximum attention to the birds speed-walking away from the incoming surf, his little body coiled with energy.

Nick and Arden watched as Jonah ran toward them but stopped short even before running out of leash.

He sat down again, vibrating with the urge to chase his prey.

"Hard to say. Depends how motivated he is."

Arden's forehead slid into a bee as she watched her dog. "I think there's more to it than that. He also needs to trust he won't drown."

Nick tilted his head toward her, taking a moment before responding. "Maybe he realizes he's better off avoiding the possibility."

Nick bent down to pick up a piece of driftwood and gave it a toss.

The pup abandoned his birdwatching and went for the stick, trotting back to where they waited with his prize between his teeth, tail held high. It didn't matter that the stick was more than half his body's length.

Nick grabbed the stick, trying to take it from Jonah's jaws.

Nothing doing. The little dog chomped down, rear end in the air, and shook his head, refusing to let Nick get a hold.

Laughing, Nick abandoned the struggle. "It's all yours, buddy."

"Thanks. I'll never get it away from him." She rolled her eyes, but her smile told Nick she wouldn't even try.

A stiff breeze coming off the water grabbed the precarious bun on top of Arden's head, loosening the scrunchie thing, and sent her hair tumbling.

She grabbed her hair with one hand, passing Jonah's leash to Nick with the other.

He took it, but used his free hand to stop her tying it back. "No, leave it down."

She looked at him from beneath her eyelids and wrinkled her nose. Nodding, she turned her face into the wind so it could blow the tangles over her shoulder.

His palms itched with the need to test the texture. He resisted temptation by balling his fist. He should have let her tie it back.

Nick turned his gaze out to sea. "You've spent quite a bit of time in Honduras, haven't you?"

Her eyes grew wary at his words. "Every summer and school holiday when I was a teenager. Why?"

"I received a call yesterday and I'd like to get your take on the problem. You have an inside perspective on the culture but are enough on the outside to be objective."

"Okay. Shoot."

"I've lost the space for the clinic. It seems there's resistance from the local leadership. While the people of the community embrace your parents and appreciate what Honduras Has Hope is doing, there are some powerful men who resent the growing American influence."

She bent to pick up a seashell and nodded. "Change always threatens people. Especially those who benefit from the status quo."

"I'm having a hard time finding another option for the clinic. Your dad has pulled strings with his contacts, but he's running up against the same resistance. It seems I may be forced to locate the clinic in a more rural location than I hoped. But the whole ministry plan is built around being in the center of the community."

They walked in silence, Nick watching the wheels turning inside Arden's head. Lately, lack of words led to awkwardness between them. This time, it was like a balm to his soul. He'd had no one to share his work with—other than those who had a vested interest. It felt good.

"Didn't you say you had a local man who was helping you in town? Don Carlos, wasn't it? What if you increased his involvement? Made him more of a front man? Maybe that would appease the local leadership."

Nick stopped in his tracks, his own wheels turning.

Arden wandered a few steps before noticing.

Of course, why hadn't he seen it? He grabbed Arden around the waist and spun her around, causing her to drop Jonah's leash.

The little dog barked and ran circles around them, loving this new game.

Giving her a loud kiss on the cheek, he set her down. "That's perfect. I can work with that." The log jam inside his brain gave way, and thoughts and ideas rushed in. Here was the breakthrough he needed.

She was smiling, but her head shook back and forth. "I don't know what you're so excited about. All I did was point out the obvious."

"It was obvious to you, not me. It seems two heads really are better than one."

The clouds covered the sun, and he noticed Arden's shiver.

Rubbing her arms as she took off at a brisk pace, she said, "Come on, let's head back and I'll make us some hot chocolate."

Before he could say anything, she looked his way, sighing with exaggerated gusto.

"Yes, I'll use fake milk and hold the marshmallows."

It was nice having someone read him so well. A little too nice. More reason to follow through on the decision he'd made. All he had to do was tell her.

He grabbed Jonah and carried him under one arm, careful not to jar the driftwood he had clamped between his teeth. "Let's go, buddy. This conversation isn't going to have itself."

ARDEN BOLDLY ADDED both whipped cream and marshmallows to her hot chocolate before handing Nick his naked version. With mugs in hand, they headed into the sitting room. Arden settled on one end of the burgundy wingback sofa while Jonah made himself comfortable at the other end. She blew on her mug before taking a sip.

Other than the kitchen, this was her favorite room in the house. A red and cream floral area rug warmed the walnut hardwood flooring. Artfully displayed red and brown accents drew one into the room, comfortable furniture kept them there. The fireplace—bordered by fully stocked, built-in bookshelves—had stacked wood begging for a match. But even a chilly day on the North Carolina coast didn't call for both a fire and hot chocolate.

A wave of accomplishment broke over her. It wouldn't be long before visitors visited Beacon Bluff, and Keeper's Quarters would welcome them with open doors and Southern hospitality.

Nick sat across from her on an overstuffed leather chair, leaning back with his ankles crossed. He lifted his drink, took a deep whiff, closed his eyes, and indulged. She heard his soft sigh. The man obviously needed more chocolate in his life.

She had to admit, she didn't hate the picture he presented—blond hair ruffled by the wind, a day's worth of stubble, and masculine hands holding his mug. It took little for her to imagine the two of them sitting here in the evening, this time with a fire going and guests sharing the adventures of the day.

*Stop right there.* How did that image sneak in? Arden leaned over to straighten the already straight magazines on the coffee table. She adjusted the angle of the floral arrangement while she was at it. Hard to have cozy after-dinner conversations while he was in Honduras and she was here.

"This is nice." Nick gestured between the two of them before continuing. "I've missed this during our mutual game of hide and seek."

"Whatever do you mean?"

Nick scoffed. "We both know that we've been avoiding each other."

She fought back the urge to run and check on a non-existent pie she theoretically had in the oven. She may have once cowed before tough conversations, but she reminded herself that the Beacon Bluff Arden didn't do so.

Tilting her chin, she met his gaze. "Why do you think that is?"

"Because, like me, you're spooked by what's between us. Maybe we should address the elephant in the room."

Telling herself yet again that she could do hard conversations, she said, "I suppose I am scared. I'm building a life of my own here and yours will be in Honduras. I don't want to fall back into the bad habit of pushing my needs aside for a man whose goals differ greatly from mine."

"And I would never want you to. That's what has me concerned."

She let thoughts flicker through her mind, then she softly smiled. "No, what has us both concerned is that we won't be able to fight it. We're worried that one of us will want to forget about what we need to do and give in to what we want to do."

He took a sip, drawing out the moment. "I've told you about Vanessa. She tried to put a wedge between me and what God called me to do. I know you would never purposely do that, but I'm afraid I might let you. And in time, I'd come to resent you. The same if you gave up Keeper's Quarters to join me with your family."

Arden frowned. "I would never want you to choose between me and your ministry." She'd lost that battle once and couldn't bear to lose again.

He set his mug on the table. "If we're not careful, we could get hurt. And I don't know about you, but I don't want to go through that again."

She nodded. "So, we stop before it goes further. Is that the plan?"

He stood and sat beside her on the sofa. "Yes, that's the plan. But as hard as I try, I'm not able to rid myself of wanting to be with you."

Arden felt the warmth coming off him in waves. She wanted to lean into it, relax against it. Instead, she scooted herself further into the corner of the sofa. "Then sitting close to me while we're alone in the house probably isn't the best idea you've had."

Nick stood and shook his head as he laughed. "You're right. Which brings me to my news. I'm moving back into Colin's house this afternoon."

Her eyes flew open wide. "What? I thought it was still torn apart with repairs. At least, that's what Colin told me." She narrowed her eyes. "Or is he wanting to stay here and continue mooching off my cooking?"

Nick chuckled. "No, it's still torn apart. But they've finished enough work that I can camp out on his floor instead of yours."

She understood his point. This would be the best plan. Not only would it put distance between them, but it would stem any gossip from them continuing to live under the same roof. Yes, Colin's presence provided some protection from the rumor mill, but as a businesswoman in a small community, she couldn't risk any appearance of impropriety. And with Nick's Faith Works interview coming up, he stood to lose even more.

So then, what was this disappointment all about? It was like a weighted blanket pressing against her shoulders. "But what about our deal? You've been a tremendous help around here, but the work isn't finished." She knew she was grasping at straws but couldn't stop herself.

"I'm not leaving you in the lurch. I'll still come by and continue to work. We've done well avoiding each other lately, haven't we?" His gaze drilled into hers, letting her know how deeply he felt.

She nodded. "And I'll keep up my end of our bargain."

"Of course." He smiled. "We're adults. We know what's at stake. Now that we've talked it through, we'll be fine." He stuck out his hand for a shake. "Partners?"

She hesitated but accepted his gesture. "Partners. But you must take Colin with you when you leave. Deal?"

"Deal."

Partners always had sparks fly from their fingertips when they shook hands. Right?

## CHAPTER 14

Roadkill would feel better than he did right now.

Shivering, Nick tucked himself farther inside his sleeping bag, thinking that even laying on a hard floor was an improvement over the struggle to stay upright. He would just have to deal with the chill seeping through his make-shift bed.

Colin came in and crouched beside his pallet. Setting a glass of water and a prescription bottle beside him, he said, "Dude, you're looking rough. I can't leave you like this."

"Go on. I'll be fine." Nick groaned from the effort of forming words. "I plan on sleeping this off."

"You've got a raging case of the flu, Nick. The doctor insisted on giving you the antiviral medication."

"That's only because I told him I had to be healthy in time for the gala next weekend."

"He obviously didn't think you would be without it. Your teeth are chattering."

"Get me another blanket." It hurt to open his eyes, but he had to make his point. "Then get out of here."

Colin hung his head, then looked back at him, concern displayed across his face. "If I weren't the keynote speaker, and

129

the group hadn't already paid my non-refundable airfare, I would stay."

"Go. I'll be fine." He had to push those last words through a coughing fit.

Glancing at his watch, Colin stood and shook his head. "I'll figure something out before I head to the airport."

Colin's mouth kept moving, spouting more words, but Nick wasn't interested. He sighed, letting sleep sweep him into the comforting arms of oblivion.

What seemed like only moments later, some harridan was poking him, with another pulling him to his feet. Didn't they know he was dying? Everyone knew to let dying men die. Was that right? Dying dogs? Sleeping dogs? Didn't matter. They needed to leave him in peace.

"Up you get. No rest for the wicked, even if they are sick."

Groaning, even with a fever-induced haze, Nick recognized that voice. "Bea, I'm not up for visitors."

"You're not up for anything, but that's about to change. On your feet, young man."

"Now, Nick, we only want to help you get better. This will be a lot easier on you if you cooperate."

"Miss Ivey? Is that you? I've always liked you."

Bea snorted. "I guess I know where I stand."

He allowed the two women to help him to his feet. They were surprisingly strong for their age. The floor shifted, and the walls shimmered, but he remained standing.

"Is he on his feet yet? The car is running, and I think I've gathered everything he needs."

Arden? Now he knew he was dying. His own personal angel had come to escort him to the pearly gates.

Her arm circled his waist and urged him forward. "We'll take it slow. One step at a time."

It took all three women to wrangle his six-foot-plus frame into Arden's SUV.

He tried to help, but even a washed up, waterlogged Jonah had more strength. He settled into the buttery leather seats and sighed.

Arden held his hand as she drove, Bea and Ivey were uncharacteristically quiet in the back seat.

Nick felt every bump and swerve on the short drive to the lighthouse.

Then Bea prodded him up some stairs with the bedside manner of a billy goat.

His head only stopped spinning when he collapsed onto a mattress. Soft sheets and a downy pillow supported his head, and a warm quilt tucked around his shoulders. He looked into his angel of mercy's eyes. They looked a lot like Arden's.

"I shouldn't be here. I moved out, remember?"

"Yea, well, that was before you collapsed at death's door. Colin called me beside himself because he had to leave town. I told him I'd take care of you."

"You didn't need to bring me here. I could have stayed at Colin's."

"You have no business sleeping on a floor. And lucky for you, they delivered my furniture yesterday. Besides, it's much easier for me to look after you if we're under the same roof."

His mind grappled for something just beyond its reach. Oh. Right. "But your reputation? The grant committee?" He did his best to sit up. "I've got to go."

She made quite the display of using only her index finger to push him back onto the pillows.

*Hmmpf.* So what? He was weak. What of it? He could still take care of himself. He had been alone for his entire adult life. It was safer that way.

"No one expects you to suffer alone. But if it makes you feel better, I've asked Bea and Ivey to move in while you're here."

Too spent to put up further resistance, he settled into the covers and closed his eyes. "I'm sure I'll be better in the morning."

He felt her adjust his pillow, then sensed her moving away. He grabbed her wrist and whispered, "Don't leave."

After a moment, he felt the edge of the mattress give and a cool hand brush aside his damp hair.

A warm, four-legged friend jumped up, licked his hand, and then settled beside him. Oblivion came to him once more, but this time, his angel's fingers tangled with his and man's best friend curled up beside him.

~

FOUR DAYS LATER, Arden knew Nick's recovery was almost complete. He was as mean as a Chihuahua taking on a Great Dane.

Even Jonah, who had only left the sick bed long enough to do his business, was nowhere to be found.

Hands on her hips, she repeated, "No. I'm not making you an egg white omelet and some nauseating green smoothie. This is not a restaurant and I'm not a short-order cook. If I were, that wouldn't be on the menu."

She settled the lap tray in front of him and pointed to the scrambled eggs with cheese, English muffin, and orange juice. "Be glad I didn't put butter on the muffin or heavy cream in the eggs."

Arden swallowed the urge to laugh at Nick's pouty face. She noticed the healthy shade of his cheeks, even through four-days' worth of blond stubble. Truth be told, she wouldn't mind nursing him for longer, even with the toddler-like tantrums.

For the first two days, Nick had been aflame with fever.

Arden had dosed him with ibuprofen and his prescribed medication, keeping a cool washcloth at the ready. She'd spooned homemade broth down his throat and, when the fever broke, changed the sheets.

Now and then, Ivey would shoo her from the room and take over.

Arden knew she was playing a dangerous game by pretending he was hers to nurse, but she couldn't help it. It was a gift she was giving herself—the gift of being needed, the gift of making a difference, the gift of loving Nick through these simple acts of service.

But these gifts came with an exorbitant price tag. The price of having to say goodbye when the time came. Unfortunately, the damage was done.

Typical of the man-child his illness had reduced him to, Nick turned his puppy-dog eyes toward her. "I'm sorry, Arden. I know I'm being miserable and ungrateful. But I'm not used to being still this long. My body is used to moving."

"And just where has all that exercise and tasteless food gotten you? Flat on your back, being taken care of." She stepped back and motioned head to toe. "As for my fueled-by-Diet-Coke-and-Doritos body, my immune system is rock solid. How's that for irony?" Her teasing brought a moment of thick silence.

Nick glanced about as if he didn't know where to look. He settled for digging into the breakfast he'd turned his nose up at. He took a sip of orange juice and regarded her once again. "I can't thank you enough for taking care of me. Even though I would have been fine by myself."

She tilted her head, not hiding her confusion. "Why would you want to be sick by yourself when others are willing and able to help?"

Nick mumbled something, so she leaned in.

"What was that?"

The scowl on his face could scrape paint from the walls. "Because I don't want to get used to it."

Against her better judgment, Arden approached and balanced on the edge of the bed, careful not to rock the tray. Instead of a vital, commanding adult, she looked into the face of the small boy who was used to being uprooted from anyplace he dared to call home.

"There's no harm in accepting human kindness, Nick."

He reached over and took her hand. "Normally, I'd agree. But with you, it's different."

Beats of silence hovered between them, above them, all around them.

Arden caught her breath, then slowly let it loose. "In what way?"

Nick's throat moved like a boa constrictor downing its dinner. "Because it will be that much harder when I leave."

Yes, his words wrenched the breath from her lungs. His words also bathed her soul with joy. She hated the wound that had spawned his insecurities, yet she relished the thought of meaning so much to him. While she loathed the reminder of his imminent departure, she was happy she wouldn't be alone in the devastating aftermath.

Did that make her a bad person? Possibly.

Probably.

Okay. Yes, it did.

She wasn't proud of her flawed woman's heart. But it came with the territory of being human and loving where she shouldn't.

Ticks coming from an antique clock bounced against the walls. Dust motes drifted in the light passing through the window.

She bit her lower lip.

Nick sighed and dropped her hand.

She broke the spell by clearing her throat. "Umm, by the way. While you were sick, Colin called and wanted me to let you know Faith Works has set your interview for next Monday."

Yet another reminder that his time in Beacon Bluff had an expiration date.

She continued. "He explained you were sick, and they said you could confirm as soon as you're well. I offered Keeper's Quarters for the meeting since Colin's place still won't be fit for visitors."

"I appreciate that." Nick released her hand and swallowed the last of the orange juice. After he set the lap tray aside, he stretched his arms above his head.

Arden's stomach tightened as he threw his head back to elongate the stretch. Were those abs peeking from beneath his t-shirt?

She jumped off the bed as if poked by a cattle prod. Moving to the other side of the room, she crossed her arms.

He pushed back the bedding and eased his legs off the bed. "I need to confirm the grant interview and touch base with my contacts in Honduras. I think I'll grab my phone and sit on the porch."

"Just don't go too far. Okay?"

Another thick moment hung in the air before she could leave the room. Their shared gaze acknowledged the deeper meaning of her words.

Her eyes confirmed she wasn't just talking about the beach. In reality, she would never ask him to stay. To turn his back on his mission. But sometimes, the heart spoke before the mind could give its opinion.

His eyes spoke of regret, disappointment, and the desire for what couldn't be.

# CHAPTER 15

"*D*r. Monroe, we have reports you have taken up residence with Ms. Gray. Are those reports true?"

And the interview had been going so well.

Nick did his best to maintain a stoic, yet pleasant, expression. He was sitting at Keeper's Quarters dining table, facing the Faith Works grant selection committee. Although with that last question, they could be mistaken for a firing squad.

There were five members on the committee, and Mrs. Tucker was by far the toughest read. The other four, including Cal Porter, had put him at ease with their warmth and intelligent questions about the origin, mission, and status of Vets Without Boundaries. Mrs. Tucker's pinched face, however, forecasted a late winter cold front.

Aware of how shifting in his seat could be interpreted, he still couldn't stop. "There was a month or so when Ms. Gray's brother and I were forced to move in after a plumbing disaster made Mr. Bennett's home unavailable. I can assure you, no impropriety took place."

Cal Porter cleared his throat. "Susan, are you aware that several other members of the committee have spoken with Colin

Bennett and he has assured us there is no cause for concern?" Cal looked toward Nick, then continued. "I, for one, have no cause to doubt these assurances."

The other members of the committee were sipping tea, blotting their lips with linen napkins, or perusing the food tray with interest. No hints as to how they felt about the topic at hand.

Arden had provided a generous tray of scones, muffins, and apple tarts. A pitcher of sweet tea, a carafe of coffee, and bottles of water sat on the mahogany sideboard. He knew she was nervous for him and had indulged in a bout of stress baking.

Mrs. Turner's lips thinned even further. "Yes, Cal, I am aware. However, I feel proper due diligence requires that we question Mr. Monroe on the matter. We owe it to the other finalists as well as Faith Works' pristine reputation to fully investigate."

Nick leaned forward, arms on the table, hoping to express his sincerity. "Mrs. Tucker, if I may add, I have utmost respect for Ms. Gray and her family. In no way would I harm their reputation, nor would I jeopardize their ministry or my standing with Vets Without Boundaries."

"From what I've been hearing about town, I also understand that you and Ms. Gray are engaged in a relationship. Is that true?"

Nick swallowed. "Not really, ma'am. When we rescued the dog on the beach, local press seemed to catch hold of the story. This town is still shaking off the effects of Hurricane Camilla, and I guess they latched onto a feel-good moment. As a result, Ms. Gray and I have had the privilege of involving ourselves in community events as a team. I guess you can say we've become friends."

"No romantic involvement?"

Nick sat silent, debating how he should answer. He wanted to be truthful, but how could he explain something he himself didn't understand? And Arden didn't deserve to have her private life laid out across the table like a five-course meal. So, he settled on the basic truth.

"We have grown close but are aware God's call takes precedence."

"Thank you, Dr. Monroe. I'm sure this line of questioning has been awkward at best. I appreciate you indulging us with your answers."

"I understand, Mrs. Tucker. I welcome any inquiries the committee may have."

Cal stood at the head of the table, bringing the meeting to a close. "Dr. Monroe, thank you for your time. Let us assure you that if we could, we would award grants to every finalist. Unfortunately, that's not possible."

"Of course." Nick stood, along with the other committee members.

Mrs. Tucker opened the pocket doors leading into the foyer, and the tension blew from the room.

Everyone oohed and ahhed over their surroundings on their way to the front door.

All Nick noticed was Arden hovering on the stairway.

ARDEN DID her best to stay away from the dining room. She really did. But could she help that polishing the oak banister was next on her list of things to do? Of course, not.

And it's not as if she could decipher any words coming from behind the door. A low mumble of voices and an occasional laugh was all she could make out. Instead of pressing her ear against the wood, Arden opted to pray for the discussion being held on the other side.

And it was a good thing.

The doors opened just as she applied beeswax to the banister. Four men and a woman preceded Nick into the hallway.

He looked up to where she perched on the stairs and threw her a wink.

That seemed like a good sign.

As the other committee members left, Cal Porter caught Arden's eye. "Good to see you again, Ms. Gray."

"Please, it's Arden. I hope your meeting went well." The words were out before she could bite her tongue. "I'm sorry. I shouldn't comment on the committee's process."

Cal chuckled. "That's quite all right, I understand. I'm sure you're eager to discover if your young man here receives the grant."

She descended the stairs, setting aside the cloth she'd been using.

Nick moved to her side. "She's my biggest fan."

"I don't mean to speak out of turn, but she would be a valuable asset on the mission field. If that's the way the Lord is leading, of course."

Both Arden and Nick smiled without speaking.

Cal looked around the hallway, his eyes lingering on the detailed woodwork and the historical portraits. "It would be a real shame to give up this lighthouse, however. Beautiful home. Beautiful location."

The implication was clear. A relationship with Nick would mean she'd have to make a choice. Lighthouse versus Honduras. Her dreams versus Nick's.

Thankfully, she and Nick had already decided that the only choice to be made was to make no choice at all. They had opted out of the game, not willing for either of them to lose.

Her smile threatened to falter. Arden knew this was the wisest course of action. But not only had her heart ignored the memo, it crumpled it up and recycled it.

Cal was looking at her, expecting some sort of answer.

"We'll cross that bridge if we get to it."

Cal looked about and noticed he was the only committee member remaining inside. "It's time for me to join the others.

Arden, give my best to your folks. Of course, I'll see you both at the gala." He shook their hands and left.

The click of the closing door brought silence to the room.

Arden wasted no time breaking it. "Well, how did it go? And by 'it', I mean the interview." Why was she rambling? Why were butterflies dive bombing her insides? It wasn't her interview.

But she knew why. After spending years burying her desire to be valued, to design her own life, her stubborn heart chose this moment to rebel. It wanted Nick, despite endangering everything she had worked toward.

Intellectually, she knew that Nick receiving the grant did not mean he was choosing Honduras over her. After all, they had agreed there was no choice to be made. But maybe if he didn't get the grant, he wouldn't be able to go. At least not right away. Maybe it would give them time to explore what was between them.

No matter how fervently she petitioned the Lord to take away her yearning for Nick, it was still there—a thick ball refusing to budge.

*God forgive me, but I don't want him to go.*

Arden's eyes stung from this new realization. Her throat constricted and her eyes widened. Now was not the time for tears. Now was the time to encourage the man she loved, no matter how much it stung.

*Love?* The thought took her breath away and refused to give it back. The floor beneath her feet suddenly felt as solid as quicksand.

She looked at him standing there, fists pushed into the front pockets of his khakis, his dark blond hair combed into business casual. She had fought the feelings for so long, but they had sneaked up on her. And they were as relentless as an ocean wave being drawn back out to sea.

Nick shrugged. "I guess the meeting went well. They asked questions about the next steps I need to take to get the ministry up and running, the status of current funding, what problems I was facing...that kind of thing."

She nodded, still not recovered from the sudden epiphany she'd experienced.

"Oh, one other thing. They asked about us. If you and I were romantically involved."

Tingles ran willy nilly across her nervous system. She took a cleansing breath. "What did you tell them?"

He shrugged. "I wanted to tell them it was none of their business, but I didn't. Instead, I assured them we both understood the situation. They didn't press for more."

"What if they had?"

Given the silence, Arden wasn't sure he would answer.

Eventually he shrugged and said, "I have no idea."

As much as she wanted to poke their feelings like a sore tooth, she was afraid. What if they confirmed there was no path? What if that discovery forced them further apart? Heaven help her, but she wasn't ready to face that yet.

Instead, she asked, "Do you feel good about your chances?"

Nick's scoff grated down her spine. "Good? You're asking me if I feel good?" He petitioned the ceiling—or maybe Heaven—and took a deep breath. His gaze stabbed her with an anger he'd never directed towards her before. "There is nothing about this process that feels good. If I lose the grant, I lose the funding. If I win the grant, I'm that much closer to leaving you."

As suddenly as it came, she saw the fight drain from his body.

Nick's voice lowered, along with his head. "How's that for a choice?"

Tears lined the bottom of her eyes. She had no words. God surely wouldn't bring them together, only to force them apart.

He jerked open the door but softly closed it behind himself.

Arden collapsed on the bottom stair and buried her head in her hands. This time, the click of the door just sounded sad.

# CHAPTER 16

$\mathcal{N}$ick stood at The Lamplighter's takeout counter watching Madge pour his coffee. Always the multitasker, she chatted with the old-timers. That's one thing he'd miss. Beacon Bluff was a community in the truest sense of the word. Whether it was Madge's car trouble, Sam's plans for his summer garden, or Harvey's bum hip, they all cared for each other.

He had to wonder what it would be like to be part of such a community. To stick around long enough for people to miss you when you're gone.

He wasn't kidding himself, though. The biggest thing he'd miss was Arden Gray. She and her rascal of a sidekick had burrowed under his skin, straight to his heart. No longer dancing around the truth, he now called his feelings by name. He was in love for the second time in his life. If he could even call his water-downed feelings for Vanessa love. What he felt for Arden? It was the real deal.

"Here you go, handsome." Madge handed him the to-go cup and a bag full of something he hadn't ordered. "I've packed you up one of those bran muffins you like from time-to-time. That tip you gave me about Bert's sciatica has really helped. Both heat and ice. Who knew?"

Sometimes medical knowledge was created equal—whether it was relieving pain in animals or humans.

"I'm glad he's feeling better." He smiled and lifted the bag in salute. "You didn't have to do this, but I will certainly enjoy it. Thank you."

"Dr. Monroe, a moment, please."

A familiar young woman with a little girl clinging to her leg interrupted Nick's progress towards the door.

"Mrs. Walsh, good to see you again. How's Goldie?" He had treated their Golden Retriever a week or so ago.

It seemed as if they were going to lose her, but she had recovered from her encounter with a hit-and-run driver.

The young woman put her hand on the top of her daughter's head. "She's doing great, thanks to you. We were just on our way to stop by your office, weren't we, Meggie?"

The girl nodded and released her hold on her mom's leg, thrusting a crumpled piece of paper toward Nick.

"Meggie, what do you say to Goldie's doctor?"

"Frank you."

Nick smiled and examined the small, hand-drawn picture of what he presumed to be a picture of Goldie, beside a stick-figure with red hair to match Meggie's. Red and pink hearts were scattered across the page.

He dropped to one knee, meeting the little girl's eyes and swallowing his emotions. "Do you know what I'm going to do with this?"

The little girl popped her thumb into her mouth and shook her head.

Nick reached into his pocket and then took great care, folding the paper just so.

Meggie's eyes grew big as he placed her gift inside his wallet.

"I'm going to look at it often so I can remember you and your friend Goldie. Is that okay?"

Meggie looked up at her mom, then bobbed her head. She buried her face back into Mrs. Walsh's jeans.

The young mom's eyes were misty as she led her daughter away.

Nick stood and resumed his path to the door.

Tiffany was on her way in, so he held the door for her. "Hey, Nick."

"Tiffany. Good to see you." He went to move past her, but she stopped him with a touch on the arm.

"I'm glad I can share the good news in person. Out of the fourteen dogs from your and Arden's 'To the Rescue' news segment, all but one has been adopted. And the last guy is meeting with a family today. So, fingers crossed!"

A grin split Nick's face. "That's fantastic. Arden will be happy as well."

Tiffany's face assumed a thoughtful expression. "You know, the two of you have made a difference in the area's animal rescue space. Arden has come so far from the day we interviewed on the beach. Her kindness jumps out of the TV screen now."

"She's great, isn't she?" Watching her flourish had been one reason he'd fallen in love with her.

"The two of you make a great team. You should think about making that a full-time thing." Tiffany winked over her shoulder on the way to the counter.

Arden. Beacon Bluff. Full time.

If wishes were puppies, he'd have a kennel full.

Gala day had finally dawned. Arden stretched in her bed, disrupting Jonah's beauty sleep. Butterflies inside her stomach had also heard her phone's alarm and were now taking off.

Despite the futility of wishing for a future with Nick, she resolved to enjoy the day and not stew in the dread of what was down the road. There was no way to un-ring the bell of falling in love. Since a broken heart was inevitable, why not indulge her fantasies? Were there degrees of heartbreak? Why not enjoy the ball before the clock struck midnight?

She and Nick had passed the days since his grant interview as if nothing earth-shattering had been said between them. They seemed to agree that nothing good could come from exploring that conversation.

Arden pushed back thoughts that threatened to suffocate her excitement. If she couldn't have Nick, she would at least have memories of a perfect evening to wrap around herself when the icy winds of loneliness and isolation blew in. She would replace the harsh memories Lincoln had bequeathed her with Nick's warm gaze and the feel of his even warmer arms.

Jonah ran up and down the bed, sniffing the air.

The comforting smell of bacon brought another smile to Arden's face. Mom was awake and in the kitchen.

Her parents had arrived late last night and had stumbled into their bed without seeing much of the house.

Arden couldn't help but wonder if they had noticed the fresh flowers in their room, or the pitcher of cold water in case they woke up thirsty.

Arden dressed in a hurry, took Jonah outside, then went into the kitchen and slid onto a bar stool.

Without turning or missing a beat, Mom said, "Good morning, darling. Pour yourself some orange juice while I finish up. Dad and Colin will be here soon. They met at the house to check on the repairs."

Arden followed instructions, assuming orange juice was code for Diet Coke. She lifted the glass to her lips and regarded her mom standing at the stove. "Good morning. Did you and Dad get a good night's sleep? You're the first to use the new mattress."

"We slept very well, thank you." An ivory tunic peaked from beneath Arden's well-worn "Kiss My Grits" apron. The jangle from a bevy of bangles accompanied pancakes flipping on the griddle.

Elegance, thy name is Lila.

Mom looked about the kitchen after placing the overflowing platter on the counter. "Lovely room, by the way. And I love what you've done with this kitchen. A cook's fantasy, for sure."

Arden sipped her drink. "Thanks. I didn't need to do anything in here. The foundation's CEO had already renovated this room before having to sell."

Mom shuddered. "Ah yes, the embezzler. Every non-profit's nightmare."

The front door slammed open, setting Jonah off into a frenzy of barking.

"Something smells good! Must be Mama in the kitchen." Colin barged in, picking his mom up in a bear hug.

Laughing, she shoved his shoulder. "Put me down or I'll never finish getting this breakfast on the table."

Colin promptly obeyed. "Wouldn't want that."

Arden smiled. "Good morning, Dad. Looks like you've made a friend."

Her dad held a wriggling Jonah. He leaned his head back, trying to dodge the dog's enthusiastic face wash. "I told him I already had a shower this morning, but he seems to think I've missed a spot or two." He adjusted his hold so Jonah couldn't reach his face. "By the way, great water pressure you have here."

Such a dad comment. Still, nothing about the massive work she had done. But to be fair, they had not seen it in its original condition.

Mom hustled to the table, carrying a gravy boat full of perfect-temperature maple syrup and the platter of pancakes.

Arden followed with a bowl of scrambled eggs and a plate of Jenga-tower biscuits.

Colin had already snatched a piece of bacon and reached for a cinnamon roll. Mom had outdone herself, making everyone's favorites, even though there was no way they could make a dent in all this food.

After about a half hour, Arden stood and grabbed the coffee pot to refill her parents' mugs. After sitting back down, she observed her family from behind her glass of Diet Coke. A flashback filter dropped in front of her eyes and sepia-toned images played like an old-time movie. She saw her mom reach up and brush a biscuit crumb from her dad's chin. Colin was licking cinnamon roll icing from his fingertips. She even saw herself as a young girl, twisting her ponytail while waiting to go to the beach.

How she missed these people. Could she find her way back? On her terms this time? She knew her home was in Beacon Bluff, opening the lighthouse for others to enjoy. But did that mean she had to isolate herself from her family? Avoiding their ministry had also meant avoiding them. She was tired of sacrificing the good times to avoid the not so good.

Then there was Honduras. She had done an admirable job walling off her connection to that country following her parents' defection. But the fact of the matter was, talking with Nick about Vets Without Boundaries had reminded her of the love she felt for Honduras as a whole, as well as the people H3 served.

Maybe it was time to reevaluate the relationship with her parents. And her relationship with H3.

Mom stood and took her plate to the sink. "You know the rules, the boys are on clean-up. Arden, you and I have a manicure appointment."

Arden rinsed her plate and looked at her mom. "We do?"

"We do. Now let's get going."

Arden was on her way to gather her jacket and handbag when the doorbell rang. By the time she made it to the front door without a frenzied Jonah tripping her, there was no one there.

Hearing the crunching gravel, she glanced down the drive and saw Nick's pickup pulling onto the road. He waved but kept going. Odd.

Jonah snuffling about her feet drew Arden's attention downward. The little dog picked up a long-stemmed red rose from the porch and trotted inside.

Hmm. Arden opened the accompanying card.

I'll pick you up at 7:00.

Arden hugged the card, right above her heart. With a wide smile, she went back inside, calling after Jonah. "Hey, bring back my rose!"

# CHAPTER 17

$\mathcal{N}$ick stopped his truck in front of Arden's home, straightening his bow tie in the cracked rearview mirror. He had detailed the interior in preparation for tonight, but Ole Red couldn't be more than he was. And neither could Nick.

His time with Arden was running out. Honduras was calling to him, regardless of whether he was awarded the Faith Works grant. If he wasn't, he had faith the Lord would provide in His time. There was no doubt in his calling, so there was no doubt in his leaving.

But what about his feelings for Arden? The devil on his shoulder whispered in his ear, taunting him with what could be. But the angel on the other side reminded him that there was no happiness separate from God's will.

God forgive him, but he wanted one magical night with Arden—a night where it could just be two people joined by their feelings. What was one more memory he would have to forget?

Although left unsaid, Nick knew Arden returned his love. Her lips may have never uttered the words, but her eyes did. And the way she leaned into him whenever they accidentally touched each other. Her gentleness when she nursed him through the flu —even if he had turned into a cranky man-child. Bottom line? This woman made him feel loved. She made him feel like he was home. He'd never felt that before.

But he couldn't ask her to abandon Beacon Bluff to join him in Honduras. If he did, she might say yes. Then he'd be no better than her late husband.

Oh, for a while, they would be happy. Blissfully so. But how long would it be before she came to resent him and Vets Without Boundaries? His mom loved his dad, but that love hadn't stopped her from desperately trying to find her place. As much as his dad had tried, there had always been an underlying sense of sadness, until they retired to Florida. Only then did she flourish, discovering who she was created to be.

He couldn't ask that of Arden. He wouldn't. She had spent most of her life resenting her parents' ministry, even to the point where she jumped into an inadvisable marriage to get away from it. He couldn't allow the pendulum to swing in the other direction, where she forced herself to accept his ministry, tamping down her resentment and allowing it to fester.

Muffled barks drew him from his thoughts. Jonah had detected his presence. With one last look in the mirror, he tossed his troubled thoughts into the back of his truck. He'd unload them another day.

Looking in the mirror, Arden wanted to throw up. Lincoln's voice haunted her to this day, echoing in her ears:

*"You're wearing that?"*

*"Can't you tame that mess you call hair?"*

*"You've been skipping workouts, I see."*

The image in the mirror had trembling lips and slouched

posture. The woman staring back at her was full of doubt and unfulfilled dreams.

That woman was not her.

Arden straightened her shoulders and applied her lipstick. Lincoln's opinions had no place here. Arden substituted his words with her own.

*"This dress is beautiful."*

*"My hair sets me apart, and that's a good thing."*

*"Girl, all that walking Jonah on the beach has paid off. Your skin is glowing."*

She had decided to wear a specific dress. It was one she had bought during her marriage in a rare fit of rebellion. Of course, she never had the nerve to wear it. Lincoln would have pitched a fit until she changed her clothes. He would have considered this flowing number too Bohemian. And not in a good way.

But Arden knew it suited her—both inside and out. The dress was a soft seafoam green, with chiffon falling into layers from her waist to the floor. Clear rhinestones danced across the fabric, catching the light as she moved. It featured an illusion bodice, covered in various shades of sea foam and clear seed beading. The straight neckline stretched into capped sleeves, inviting attention to her collar bone and toned arms.

It was just a bonus that Lincoln would have hated it.

A tap against her bedroom door announced her mom's presence. "Darling, you look exquisite."

She smiled through the mirror, admiring her mom's bronze gown. Gliding into the room, Mom pressed her cheek against Arden's, careful not to muss their makeup. "Mom, that dress is gorgeous on you."

Her mother smiled her thanks. Touching the delicate necklace at Arden's throat, she said, "That's from Lincoln, isn't it?"

Looking back at the mirror, Arden regarding the diamond choker around her neck. "Yes. It's a shame to keep something so beautiful locked away just because it came from him."

"Well, it's perfect with that dress and I'd like to think you wearing it is a sign that you've moved on."

Meeting her mom's gaze in the mirror, Arden smiled. "I guess it is."

Jonah's frenetic barking alerted them to Nick's arrival.

Mom squeezed Arden's hand. "Your father and I will see you at the gala."

Arden took a moment to close her eyes and rest a hand over her stomach. A few deep breaths.

No matter what happened tonight, God was in control. He already knew the grant recipient's identity and what the future held.

She heard the muffled voices of her parents greeting Nick on their way out the door.

Jonah trotted into the room, jumped up on the bed, and settled into the pillows. He watched from his perch as she gathered her clutch and moved to the bed. He tilted his head and offered a soft "woof," as if sensing the big night ahead.

Arden gave his chin a scratch and turned off the lamp. "Don't wait up."

# CHAPTER 18

$\mathcal{A}$rden's skin prickled with excitement as Nick drove up the circular drive to the Coastal Carolina Yacht Club.

He tossed the keys to a valet. "Take good care of him. He's a classic."

Arden couldn't rein in her laugh. Her pumpkin had turned into an old pick-up truck, and she wouldn't have it any other way.

Nick acknowledged her reaction with a grin. "Ole Red is older than that kid. I'm sure he hasn't had the privilege of driving such a rare specimen of automotive excellence."

Stepping into the lobby on Nick's arm, the rarefied atmosphere mocked her. As if it knew she didn't fit in. In days past, with Lincoln as her escort, she would have agreed. But now she knew better. She was a daughter of the one true King, and no one—not even herself—could refute her right to fit in anywhere she chose to be.

Portraits of stuffy men in nautical garb looked down their noses, and pretentious design renderings of what Arden presumed to be notable vessels celebrated the wealth of their owners. Gilded trophy cups preened behind locked glass-front cabinets. But the *pièce de résistance* was the five-foot sculpted captain's wheel taking center stage, decorative lighting making it glow with importance.

A low whistle came from Nick's lips. "I'm not sure mere mortals are qualified to breathe the air in here."

"Mom said it was the one place in the area that could justify the exorbitant per-plate cost of the gala. She's hunting the big guns with thick wallets."

"She's a force to be reckoned with."

Arden rolled her eyes. "That she is."

Two formally dressed servers framed the ballroom doors. They handed Nick and Arden crystal flutes of non-alcoholic champagne. Thanks to her time with Lincoln, she had been to more elegant, meant-to-impress events than she could remember. Even so, she was captivated by what greeted her across the threshold.

Alternate colors of billowing tulle—royal blue, gold, and white—draped the ceiling. Fairy lights glittered through the fabric, setting the illusion of a night beneath the stars. Each table was covered with a royal blue tablecloth, topped with white china, gold utensils, and crystal water goblets. Blooming mounds of white baby's breath in gold trumpet vases stood tall in the center of each table, surrounded by white pedestal candles. The back of each banquet chair was wrapped with royal blue velvet, gathered with a posy bouquet of white roses, baby's breath, and gold ribbon.

Nick cleared his throat and swiped a hand across the back of his neck. "Good thing I'm a finalist or they wouldn't let me in. Ole Red wouldn't have made it past the valet stand."

She gave him a wink. "Don't worry, I would have smuggled you in. I have some pull with the hosts."

Waitstaff circled with silver trays of phyllo brie puffs, blueberry goat cheese crostini, tuna tartare, and other assorted small bites.

Nick inspected the sample he nabbed from the tray. "Do I want to know what I'm eating?"

She glanced at the small bite and waited for him to pop it into his mouth. "I hear caviar is quite nutritious. But the cracker is full of carbs."

Nick's eyes got as round as sand dollars and his chewing slowed. Closing his eyes, he swallowed, chasing the fish eggs with a gulp of sparkling beverage.

Arden smothered the giggle, but she couldn't disguise her grin.

Shuddering, he said, "You could have warned me." He wasn't able to hold his glare long before his face broke out in a self-deprecating smile.

"And miss the show? Not a chance."

He nodded at a passing tray. "Nothing for you?"

She waved off his question. "I prefer grape jelly meatballs and mozzarella sticks."

"Good luck finding those here."

Arden placed her empty glass with others on a tray being circulated by the ever-efficient waitstaff. She studied the hardbound commemorative book handed to her earlier. The substantial weight of the book informed the reader that its contents were worth the time it would take to read through it. The royal blue leather-like cover had Faith Work's logo embossed in gold, along with the verse "Faith Without Works Is Dead. James 2:26"

Arden flipped past the welcome pages, the history of the Faith Works Foundation, updates on previous grant winners and then found what she was looking for. She nudged Nick's elbow with her own. "Look at this guy. I'd trust him with grant money, wouldn't you?"

Nick pulled at his collar and shifted his weight.

She had stopped at the page with a full-color photo of Nick with his arms around several Honduras villagers, three dogs sitting at their feet.

The breath caught in her throat at the sheer joy radiating off the page. Nick's eyes were glowing, the corner crinkles deeply etched as he looked straight at the camera. He didn't just have his arms around the two men by his side, he was grabbing them close like brothers.

Nick always had a quick smile, but never had she seen him with the one he had on that day, at that location. One of the dogs looked up at him, a goofy grin on its face, tongue hanging out.

His smile had the power to impact her like no other. Her finger traced his lips on the page, but then a raspy throat clearing drew her attention.

Well, that was embarrassing. Being caught caressing your date's face on a photograph...by said date.

Her cheeks heated, but she slanted him a look with a raised eyebrow, punctuated with an impish grin. "Cute pooch."

As if she was petting the dog in the picture. Yeah, right.

Despite her playfulness, a tightness moved up her throat. While his handsome face had jumped off the page, drawing her attention—and wayward fingers—Arden couldn't deny the wide smile on his lips or the undeniable glow in his eyes.

It was obvious. Nick was in his element.

She skimmed the description of Vets Without Boundaries, its mission, and its needs. She lifted her gaze to Nick, who had been watching her, and she laid a hand on his forearm, feeling his muscles tense.

"I'm so proud of you." Her voice was thick, her smile trembling.

"Oh no you don't. You are not going to get emotional. This is a night of celebration—of all the good God is doing in the world through all these amazing charities." He took the book from her and led them to their tables.

Arden had a spot at H3's table, and Nick was at the table reserved for finalists.

He took the book from her and set it at her place, helped her off with her wrap, and placed her clutch on her seat. Grabbing Arden's hand, he towed her across the room.

He stopped at the open French doors and looked into her eyes. "And we're going to laugh, be happy, and enjoy each other. Even if it kills us."

They stepped out onto the patio where the canopy of string lights cast their glow on the glittering dancers.

Her mother had disguised the army of propane patio heaters behind potted plants, providing a comfortable oasis from the cool March breeze. The ocean wasn't far away, and the moon over the water lit a pathway to the horizon. The five-piece band her mother had brought in from Atlanta sat off to the side, providing an upbeat soundtrack for the evening.

"There's my girl!" Dad claimed Arden's hand and quirked an eyebrow at Nick. "You don't mind if I steal her, do you?"

"Of course not, sir." He touched Arden's elbow. "I see some people I should catch up with. Find me when you're done?"

She nodded, following her dad to the dance floor. Slipping into his arms, she felt like a little girl again, standing on his shoes while he danced her around the kitchen. She kissed him on the cheek. "I love you, Daddy."

He squeezed her waist. "Pumpkin, I love you too." He swung her around in a practiced move, then continued. "You know, I'm so proud of you. Many have stumbled after experiencing the trials you have. But I see your strength, your personal growth, and admire what you're doing here in Beacon Bluff."

So much for not becoming emotional this evening. The warmth of a thousand candles spread throughout her insides, his words more valuable than any expensive bauble Lincoln had ever gifted her.

"I've stumbled plenty."

"But you're still standing. That's what counts." He kissed her forehead, and they settled into the dance.

She scanned the crowd for Nick, finding him talking with an

older couple she recognized. The Fontaines were delightful, and their heart for missions were well known. Another couple stopped and claimed Nick's attention. He widened the circle and laughed at whatever the gentleman had said.

Arden realized that, despite what he'd said earlier, he was equally comfortable in this elegant setting as he had been in the picture. Wealthy tuxedoed donors or salt-of-the-earth laborers standing on the streets of Honduras. It made no difference to Nick.

Her dad must have noticed her preoccupation. He tipped his chin toward Nick and said, "He's nothing like Lincoln, you know."

Arden sighed. "Truer words were never spoken."

"Your mother and I believe we played a role in pushing you into that marriage. And, while I have no standing to dictate your life choices, I would encourage you to take a closer look at Nick Monroe."

"No closer look is needed, Daddy. But I'm afraid God is calling us in different directions."

"Be very careful in discerning God's call, pumpkin. Often, our human failings blur the lines of God's truth."

The music ended and her dad escorted her back to Nick's side.

Nick slid his arm around her waist and drew her into the conversation.

They enjoyed the hors d'oeuvres that weren't caviar and took advantage of the various carving stations tucked off to the side.

Good food, friendly conversation, good laughs. And Nick by her side.

Finally, when there was a lull in the folks seeking their company, Nick drew her close. "I've missed you."

"What do you mean? Except for the one dance with my dad, I've been right here."

"You and scads of other people." The band struck up a

romantic ballad, and Nick tugged her toward the path leading to the beach. "Come with me."

Like two mischievous children escaping their parents' notice, they scooted down the path.

Laughing, Arden held on to Nick's arm and removed her shoes, dangling the straps between her fingers. She dropped them, however, when Nick pulled her into his arms and began to dance.

"I can still hear the music, can you?"

The cool sand tickled her toes and Arden shivered.

Nick ran a hand along her arm, bending his face until she felt his warm breath against her face. "Cold?"

She pulled back a bit, looked him in the eye, and shook her head. "Not at all."

He stopped dancing long enough to open his tux jacket and tuck her inside. He kissed her forehead. "Just to make sure."

She curled back into his warmth as he resumed their dance, winding her arms around his waist. Resting her cheek on his chest. Not thinking. Just feeling.

Their steps moved across the sand to the distant strains of the orchestra. But as the music faded, so did their pretense. They held onto one another, swaying to music of their own making. Moonlight rolled through the waves, the hum of their ebbing and flowing insulating them from reality.

Inevitably, his lips met hers. It was a given that she would tighten her arms and surrender to the bliss.

His hands cupped her face, his thumbs caressing her cheeks. He tilted her head, giving him better access to her lips, and a groan rose from within her very soul.

Her lower lip was a perfect fit between both of his.

He nudged his lips into the welcoming softness, sending shivers down her spine that had nothing to do with the weather. He broke away only to pepper her cheeks with tender kisses.

The kiss ended with him breathing deeply and erratically. He rested his forehead against hers and whispered, "You know I love you, don't you?"

Her heart burst into millions of pieces of light, joining the stars above, sparks falling around them. Sizzle tripped along her nerve endings, sparking flames of utter joy. "I love you too. So much."

They grinned at each other, happy to have their feelings out in the open.

But clouds came through, masking the moon and stars, extinguishing the light. The mood shifted from one of joy to one of uncertainty.

Nick's eyes lost some of their shine, so she knew he felt it too.

Her eyes misted, and Nick groaned, pulling her even closer.

"What are we going to do?" Her words may have been soft, but they shattered the heavy silence.

He ran his fingers along the nape of her neck, tangling in the mass of curls. "I don't know. But somehow, someway, we need to work this out without either one of us backing away from what we need to do."

She nodded, worried that this was beyond them. But there was no hurry. Surely, they could pray and find a path they could walk together.

They heard the pounding steps coming down the path, and they sprung apart. Colin came into view, trying to catch his breath. "There you are. They're preparing to introduce the grant finalists and announce the winner."

Before moving to follow her brother, Nick took her hands. "No matter what the outcome, just remember, I love you, and I believe we were meant to meet that day you stumbled across Jonah."

She squeezed his hands and nodded. Picking up her abandoned shoes, she gave him a smile. "Let's go. It's time for you to take the stage."

Nick escorted her to her table where Cal Porter and her

family sat. She took her seat between her mom and Colin, while Nick went to sit with the other four finalists, greeting each one with a handshake, a smile, and good wishes.

Arden's mind checked out while dinner was served. Afterward, Cal, her dad, and Colin took turns introducing video montages of each ministry represented in the finals. Amidst the muted video narrations, applause, and clinking of waitstaff clearing glasses and plates, Arden was brimming with ambivalence.

Vets Without Boundaries deserved the funding, but so did the other ministries. If another ministry won, would Nick be more inclined to stay stateside for a while longer? Giving them time to become a couple and chart a future together?

A hush spread across the room, the absence of sound interrupting Arden's thoughts.

Cal stepped up to the podium, an award-show style sealed envelope in his hand. He cleared his throat, said something about all finalists deserving of the honor, etc., etc.

"The winner is..." He opened the envelope, paused, and looked over the audience, his gaze eventually stopping at the table of finalists. Cal stretched the silence, milking the suspense for all he was worth.

"Congratulations, GAL516! May this money aid your fight against human trafficking."

Arden's gaze latched onto Nick.

He jumped up and shook the GAL516 representative's hand as others applauded. Nick kept a smile on his face throughout the woman's acceptance speech and kept his head bowed and eyes closed throughout the closing prayer.

Yes. She'd peeked.

As soon as everyone began to disperse, she pushed her way through the crowd, rushing to the finalists' table. She needed to get to Nick. She needed to make sure he was okay.

After taking a few elbows to the ribs and having been shoved this way and that, Arden finally laid her eyes on Nick, one table away.

Yes, many of the people were there to congratulate the winner, but the other finalists were garnering a fair amount of attention as well. Well-wishers surrounded Nick and she couldn't get any closer.

She stood on her tiptoes, looking over shoulders, hoping to catch his eye. When she did, her heart sank to the bottom of her stomach.

His eyes were empty, despite the smile and cheerful words coming from his mouth. No one else would notice the lack of his inner spark, but she did.

He broke their gaze and said something quickly to the person he was speaking with. He turned toward her, and the sea of people parted for him as he made his way to her side.

She knew now was not the time or place for any sympathetic words or embrace. Too many watchful eyes, too many distractions.

So, she simply said, "Are you okay?"

He shrugged, not meeting her eyes. "I'm good." He glanced back over his shoulder. "Hey, I need to get back. I hate to ask this, but do you think you could ride home with your folks?"

Her face froze in place, but her legs trembled. "Of course. You do what you need to do here."

Nick waved to someone over her shoulder before saying, "I'll catch up with you later."

He turned away, and the crowd swallowed him whole.

No smile. No reassuring touch. No Nick. Had he just blown her off?

Arden's blood ran cold, chilling the rest of her body. It was at that moment she realized that more than bodies stood between them. There was a chasm now, where before they had shared the same air. It had taken less than an hour for her to tumble from the mountaintop to the valley of despair.

Arden stumbled backward into someone. Mumbling her apologies, she found Colin and asked him to take her home. Her parents were catching up with old friends and she didn't want to intrude or interrupt their evening.

Colin frowned. "You don't look so good. Where's Nick?"

Arden rubbed her forehead. "I'm fine, just a sick headache coming on. Nick will be tied up for a while, and I don't want to pull him away."

She saw a smart retort pass across his face, but he caught himself before saying anything. "Sure, come on. I'll take you home, then I can come back to finish up here."

She nodded. The Barbie doll smile she had perfected during her marriage was in place. Her shell of composure, however, was about to crack, spilling all her painful, twisted insides onto the floor for all to see. She had to leave.

Colin turned to her as they waited for the valet to bring his car around. "If he's hurt you, I promise you he'll answer to me." Her brother's voice was harsh, ragged with anger. "Tell me what he's done."

"Please, Colin, not right now. I just can't." She had so little energy, her voice barely qualified as a whisper.

For once, her brother gave her the emotional space she craved. Colin's arm around her shoulders helped her find strength as they stood in silence.

On the drive home, they exchanged a couple of inane observations on the lovely evening. Colin gripped the steering wheel, but he allowed her to mourn in silence.

The clock had struck midnight, and her prince was nowhere to be found.

# CHAPTER 19

*N*ick cut the engine and sat back in his seat. Keeper's Quarters loomed above him, its light circling through dark. It would take much more than this manmade source of light to guide him to safety.

He rubbed the back of his neck. What a mess. Not only had he gone and fallen in love with Arden Gray, but he had the bad judgment to tell her. Not only had he created his own mess, but he'd also dragged Arden into it as well.

Losing the grant had been a five-alarm wake-up call, jarring in its intensity. Oh, Vets Without Boundaries would be fine and move forward in better shape than he thought possible. As it turned out, the ministry had gained widespread exposure just by being a finalist. A handful of five-star donors had met with him after the gala and pledged their financial support.

It was the reason he had lost the grant that ate at him. Cal had pulled him aside, assuring him he had been in the final running. The decision came down to a couple of factors, including the fact that he had the support of the Bennett family. Other ministries didn't have access to such a network and could arguably benefit more from Faith Works' support.

Even without that consideration, Cal wasn't sure the decision would have gone Nick's way. The committee was concerned that he and Arden had been sharing the house, although they believed nothing improper had taken place. But facts often had little to do with ministries falling from grace. Faith Works ultimately decided they could not risk even the appearance of impropriety.

Nick pounded a fist against the steering wheel and the reverberating pain was well-deserved. Had he learned nothing from Vanessa? Relationships and ministry don't mix. He had turned his back on that lesson by allowing himself to develop feelings for Arden.

From the moment she had cried in his arms over an injured dog that day in the clinic, instinctively he had known his heart was at risk. Arrogance had made him believe he could control his feelings, keep Arden at a safe distance. Like Jonah's namesake, he ignored what he knew God was telling him.

Vanessa hadn't loved him enough to share his goals. Arden was dead set against having anything to do with her parents' work in Honduras. While the two women were as different as night and day, the endgame had been identical. It didn't matter that his immature love for Vanessa was far removed from this bone-deep love he felt for Arden. Nick still stood alone.

But standing alone is what he did best. Hadn't he learned how from a young age? Nick remembered one time in particular when he was a freshman in high school. He had just been named the school's starting quarterback. Eager to share his triumph at the dinner table, he had rushed home after practice. He announced the news, happiness all but spilling onto the table. He had expected his parents to be excited and proud. He had expected a family celebration.

Instead, his parents had exchanged looks and his father had laid down his fork, straightening the cutlery. Nick's dinner had worked way up to his throat. His dad hadn't needed to say a word. He knew.

Lashing out at his father, he had demanded to know why he kept doing this to his family. Why could they never stay put and enjoy a normal life? Tears had traveled down his mother's cheeks as she clutched a napkin to her lips. Couldn't his dad see what he was doing to them?

He hadn't scolded Nick for his impertinence or his anger. Nick could still see the compassion and sorrow in his eyes as he had explained that God had put a call on his life. And when He did, He knew the consequences that his family would face and had already factored that into Nick's future. That while Nick couldn't see it, understand it, or even want it, God would work it all together for Nick's good.

He had gone to bed that night, but never closed his eyes, counting the nubs on the popcorn ceiling. His mind wrestled with his disappointment, trying to reconcile his father's words with the desire for a normal life. By the time morning seeped through the crack in his curtains, he had made his peace with God. If God was going to turn his vagabond childhood into good, Nick wouldn't fight it.

He should have never tried out for the football team to begin with, knowing what his father did for a living. But the lure of belonging to a team, being one of the guys, had been too strong. They had only been at their current church for a year, and he had been so sure they would stick around for at least one football season.

He should have known better than to second-guess God.

Two months later, they had left, and the team had gone on to the state championship without him. And he had never touched a football again.

He needed to speak with Arden. Somehow make her understand why it wouldn't work between them, despite loving each other. The thought of hurting her stole his breath. How was he going to form the words he needed to end this?

He left the car, knowing exactly where to find her.

~

ARDEN WRAPPED herself in one of Miss Ivey's blankets, feet dangling off the gallery. The rhythm of the waves should have soothed her anxiety, but it agitated her further.

After Colin had dropped her off, she had gone to her room and picked up Jonah, cuddling him close to her face. Tears had leaked from her lashes, and she had cried softly into her boy's fur.

Instead of squirming or demanding to go outside as he normally did when she returned home, Jonah laid his head in the crook of her neck and let her love him.

Tears spent, she'd removed the dress that had filled her with such confidence. Now it lay in a crumpled heap, discarded just like her hopes for the future.

She put on her most comfortable sweats and slipped her feet into fuzzy-lined Ugg boots. Scrubbing her face clean and removing her hair clips, Arden tied her hair into a messy bun and had regarded herself in the mirror. A far cry from the woman who had stood there only hours before.

Now, with the ocean at her feet and the heavens above, she concentrated on her breathing. She had no chance of making sense of her life with her mind in turmoil. In. Out. In. Out.

The echo of the metal door banging closed and the subsequent footsteps climbing the staircase made a mockery of her search for peace.

She focused on the whitecaps as if she didn't notice Nick stepping out onto the balcony. At least he kept his distance, leaning his hands onto the railing looking straight ahead, as if the darkness held the answers to what lay between them.

It didn't. She had already looked.

"I'm sorry for tonight," he said.

She shrugged one shoulder. "You need to be more specific."

He dropped his head between his outstretched arms, saying nothing.

"Here, let me help you out. Are you sorry for leaving me high and dry at the gala? Or are you sorry for shutting me out after what had to be one of your biggest disappointments in life? Maybe you're sorry for telling me you loved me." Her voice choked on her last words.

His silence spoke volumes.

"That's it, isn't it?"

That shook him out of his trance. He turned his head, eyes blazing with pain. "I do love you. But I never should have told you."

Arden scrambled to her feet, the blanket dropping away along with her tenuous composure. She shoved him so hard he fell back against the brick wall. "Why are you doing this? Why are pushing me away? You know how I feel about you." Her throat worked to keep sobs from escaping. "I love you, Nick. And I know you love me."

Anger battled despair across his face. "Don't you see? God has put a calling on my life and I can't walk away from it."

"Who's asking you to? Not me!"

"And I won't ask you to leave Beacon Bluff."

Following his outburst, silence froze the air between them.

She picked up the blanket and wrapped it around herself once more, as if it could stop the ice forming inside her heart. "You're leaving for Honduras, aren't you." A statement of fact. Not a question.

He nodded. "Tomorrow." His throat worked around the words that further shattered her world. "I booked the flight before I came over. No sense in drawing this out for either of us."

"You won't even try to work this out?"

He shook his head. "There's no use. We're at a dead end, Arden."

There was no holding back the sobs now. "So maybe you're sorry for leading me on. Hmm?"

"I'm guilty of leading us both on." Anguish. Regret. It was all spread across his face. "I was foolish to think maybe we could handle these feelings between us."

Just as she had when they first met over Jonah's rescue, she lost control and made a fool of herself by crying in front of this man. She wanted to be stoic. She didn't want this to be their last memory together. But it hurt too much.

"I never meant to hurt you." His voice was thick. He brought her to his chest, his cheek pressing against hers. His silent tears mingled with hers, his uneven breathing joining hers.

Eventually, the storm eased, and they simply held each other. Unable to do otherwise and despite the reality of what was to come, she relished his arms around her this one last time.

He pulled away just enough to kiss her forehead and brush tendrils of hair from where tears stuck them to her face. "Let me walk you downstairs."

Finally removing herself from his arms, she shook her head, her mind made up. "No. Just go. It's better if we end it here."

He inhaled a shaky breath and rubbed his palm across his eyes, pinching the bridge of his nose. Regret palpated between them, almost changing her mind. A few more minutes couldn't make this pain any worse, could it?

But she stood resolute. The thought of going down 129 steps with him watching her every move made her want to be sick. Just imagining him driving away in that wonderful, beat-up truck made her want to double over. What on earth would she do if faced with the reality?

She leaned in and kissed his cheek, quickly turning her back. "God speed, Nick. You'll do great things in Honduras. I know it." Her voice broke, joining the pieces of her heart on the iron floor.

Nick moved behind her, wrapping his arms around her shoulders. His presence was like a branding iron against her back. Far too soon, he released her and moved out the door and down the stairs. And, just as quickly, the chill took over.

Dropping to her knees, she hugged herself tight. She fisted

her hand over her mouth, not wanting him to hear her keening sobs.

The ending of her marriage was nothing compared to this ending with Nick. She had survived the one, but she didn't know how she would survive this time. She looked to the night sky, seeking answers. Instead, she saw the same stars that had mocked her when her parents had left. A sulfureous reminder of the distance that would soon separate her from Nick.

*Please, Lord. Help me, one more time.*

# CHAPTER 20

*S*ince her parents had stayed at the gala deep into the early hours of the morning, no one was up and about to notice Arden only leaving her room to take care of Jonah. She spent the rest of the morning hiding under bedsheets and blankets, holding her sweet dog close.

From time-to-time he would whimper and lick tear tracks from her face. But mostly he curled under her arm, resting his chin on her shoulder. And there was no one to notice if Jonah's fur was a bit damp.

By late afternoon, Arden was heartily sick of herself. Her head ached, her eyes were a puffy mess, and her hair was a rat's nest. Maybe showering would bring her back to the land of the living, but she wasn't holding her breath.

But at least it would drown the sound of her sobs.

Forcing herself to focus on the mundane rituals of self-care, it wasn't until she had pulled on some jeans and a sweater that a sickening thought crept back in.

Was Nick on the plane right this very minute?

That horrible wave of pain flooded every nook and cranny of her body.

Ever sensitive to her emotions, Jonah hopped up and pawed her leg.

Arden picked him up, drying her tears in his absorbent fur. "I know, boy, this has to stop."

She opened the bedroom door, determined to regain control.

Arden stepped into the kitchen and froze. Her mother sat at the table, coffee in hand, scrolling through her phone. At the sound of Arden's footsteps, she glanced up and smiled.

Arden wasn't fit for company, but turning and bolting would only invite more questions. She'd power through. Somehow.

She opened the refrigerator and stifled a gag at the mere sight of food. When she turned around, her mom was just behind her, setting her coffee cup in the sink.

Her mother looked at her, kindness and love shining in her eyes. "How are you holding up, darling? Colin told me Nick is heading to Honduras today."

Faced with her mom's compassion, Arden's resolve evaporated. She flung herself into her mom's hug, choking on her feelings once again. "Oh, Mama. It hurts so bad."

Her mother rubbed her back and murmured the universal phrases moms say to their hurting children. Be it a skinned elbow or a broken heart, the soft words work like magic.

Arden pulled away, reaching for a tissue. "Sorry, Mom. I didn't mean to slobber all over your blouse."

"You can slobber on me anytime, Arden. Honestly, I wish I'd been there for you after Lincoln's death—even if it meant getting slobbered on."

Arden shrugged. Needing to do something with her hands, she went back to the fridge and took out a Diet Coke. "You and Dad were in the middle of that pastor's conference. I understood you had responsibilities. Colin was there, and you did make it for the funeral."

Her mom gave a brief chuckle. "Your brother is many things,

but maternal isn't one of them. I'm afraid prioritizing my responsibilities didn't win me any mom-of-the-year awards." Mom approached Arden and smoothed stray curls from her face. "Will you forgive me? For all the times you needed me, and I wasn't around?"

Despite the raw sting from her earlier tears, fresh ones slipped down her cheeks. Where were they all coming from? She should be dehydrated by now.

"Mama, I need to apologize," she said, her voice thick with emotion. "I'm so sorry for being angry and resenting your work in Honduras. All it did was push me further away from you. After Lincoln was gone, I was so determined to make it on my own. I didn't feel like I had anyone else to lean on." She reached out, gently touching her mother's cheek to soften the weight of her words.

Her mother clutched both of Arden's hands. "You owe me no apology. You played the hand your father and I dealt you." She pulled her to the kitchen table.

They sat across from each other, gripping each other's hands as if they could make up for lost time by sheer force.

"Your father and I were so preoccupied with building the Honduras ministry we ran roughshod over your feelings. We believed we were leaving you in excellent hands with the Grays, but I'm afraid all we did was push you into an unfortunate marriage. Maybe if we'd been around, we could have steered you in a different direction. I'm not sure I'll ever be able to forgive myself for abandoning you like we did."

It was Mom's turn to burst into sobs. "I missed your senior prom!"

Arden couldn't help but chuckle despite the moisture spilling from her eyes. "That's what you regret?"

"I was so jealous that Sharon helped you pick out a dress, take you to hair and nail appointments, and buy the right shoes. I wanted to be the one to shepherd you through that exciting rite of passage. I cried over those pictures for days."

Hearing those words of regret shifted something in Arden's heart, and forgiveness swept in and replaced the pain and anger where her mother was concerned.

Arden wiped away what had turned into sweet tears of reconciliation. "Well, I have forgiven you and you know God has. So maybe you should, too?"

Her mother hugged her tight. "When did you get to be so wise?"

Arden sat back in the chair and sighed. "Oh, Mama. I'm not wise at all. If I were, I wouldn't have fallen for Nick, knowing he was moving to Honduras. It's like I was shaking my fist at God, daring him to take someone away from me again."

"I don't think that's what you were doing at all. I think you met a man who made you feel special, a man you could love and go through life with." Resting a hand on Arden's forearm, Mom continued. "As for the Honduras thing, are you sure it's a deal breaker?"

Arden narrowed her puffy eyes. "What do you mean?"

"Don't worry, this isn't about me guilting you into joining us in Honduras."

Arden raised an eyebrow.

"Not this time, anyway." Her mom had the grace to look sheepish. "Don't get me wrong, I love what you're doing here and I can see how it suits you. Beacon Bluff has always been your special place and what you've done here is beautiful. I'm so proud of you. I can't stand myself for ever wanting to pull you away for my own selfish reasons."

Her mom threw her arms around Arden's neck.

"Please forgive me for not telling you sooner." Mom sat back in her chair. "I should have told you the moment I walked through your door. But I was still fighting the thought that this place was what was keeping you from coming home to us. That it would bring you comfort like I never had. I now see it as nothing more than fear and jealousy. This is your home. Forgive me?"

Arden had always sought her mom's approval—most likely a byproduct of their rocky past. But this all-encompassing joy caught her by surprise. She hugged her mom close and buried her head in her neck. Like a child happy to see her parent return from a long absence.

Her mother dipped her head to better look Arden in the eye. "But does it have to be all or nothing? All Beacon Bluff or all Honduras?"

She met her mom's loving gaze. Could there be a middle ground for her and Nick? Hope flickered before sputtering. "I've given that some thought, but unfortunately, I haven't found any workable compromise. He can't treat animals in Honduras from Beacon Bluff, and I can't abandon everything I'm building here to follow him. I just can't."

"I'm not suggesting you sacrifice God's plans for your life on the altar of someone else's ministry. But be sure you're not holding onto your past as a shield to protect you from the future. Your father and I pushed you into the arms of the wrong man. Don't let what we did push you away from the arms of a good one."

"I don't know how to do that, Mom."

"Do you remember memorizing the pieces to the armor of God? Your shield needs to be one of faith. Not fear. Maybe if you're able to forgive your dad and I for hurting you, you could make room for that faith."

"Mama, even if I could figure something out, I don't know if Nick would even want me. He left without even trying to find a solution." That sick feeling in the pit of her stomach returned. "It's like he gave up. Like I wasn't worth it." She muffled a sob with her fist.

"Oh, darling. Of course you're worth it." Mom tightened her arms, punctuating her words. Her mom sat back and brushed

Arden's hair from her face. "As for Nick, I can't say whether he's given up or not. Neither can you unless you find out for sure." Kissing her daughter's cheek, she said, "One thing I do know, none of this has caught God by surprise."

Seemingly as exhausted from all their emotion as Arden was, her mother stood and brushed lint from her tailored slacks, glancing at the clock. "Let's get out of here and go buy some fresh shrimp. I'm in the mood for a good ole fashioned shrimp boil."

"Sounds perfect." Family time. That's what she needed.

Following her mom to the car, Arden was glad to close the door on all that heavy emotion. Her mind was drained, and her body exhausted.

She looked forward to sitting around a kitchen table with her family, eating shrimp, corn on the cob, potatoes, and sausage dumped onto newspaper down the middle of the table. It had been a family tradition during their summers here. And, of course, she had to make sure Colin didn't eat more than his fair share of shrimp.

She managed a slight smile, happy that she and her mother had found each other again. God was good, even in the dark times.

Despite the positives from this afternoon, Arden hadn't stopped missing Nick. There was still a Nick-sized hole in her heart, but at least now she knew she had the support of family.

NICK HELPED a woman lift her carryon into the overhead bin, then found his seat. At such short notice, no aisle seat had been available, so he folded his six-foot-plus frame into a five-foot-minus window seat. His knees jammed into the seat in front of him, aggravating an old running injury. But he suffered in silence. He didn't deserve to be comfortable after leaving Arden like he did. Cramming himself against an airplane window seemed fitting.

Based on their matching t-shirts, a short-term mission group filled the surrounding seats.

An older couple paused at the two seats beside him. The wife buckled herself in while her husband stood in the aisle, patting his pockets then digging through his small bag.

"Marilyn, I can't find my reading glasses. Alex Cross can't solve his next crime without me, you know."

Marilyn had pulled out a magazine and flipped through the pages. Without glancing at her husband—yet with a small smile—she said, "They're on your head, Bill."

He touched his hair, then settled in his seat and chuckled. "So they are. The good Lord knew what He was talking about when He said it wasn't good for man to be alone."

The couple gave each other a quick kiss then Marilyn patted Bill's knee. "It goes both ways, dear. I'm happy you're at my side."

Nick inwardly smiled, appreciating their gentle banter. But he quickly sobered. Moments such as these roused the memories of his time with Arden, deepening the pressure around his heart. Like the time she tried to teach him how to make bread.

Nick hoped the couple would entertain themselves. He wasn't fit company for anyone. Acknowledging them with a smile he inserted his earbuds, the universal do-not-disturb sign.

As the plane lifted off, Nick stared out the window, watching the ground fall away beneath him. He'd made his choice. Booked the flight. Said goodbye.

In a matter of hours, he'd be in Honduras, armed with the resources he needed to launch Vets Without Boundaries. What had felt like failure—losing the Faith Works grant—had become something else entirely. God had opened other doors, those that brought people into his path who believed in the mission enough to fund it.

So why did it feel like his heart had sunk somewhere below

his stomach, heavy and dragging? He didn't need a diagnosis. It was because he'd left Arden. Walked away and pretended it hadn't gutted him. But it had. And the ache of it hollowed him out with every step, thought, or breath that reminded him of her absence.

He hadn't had a choice. Right? Her life was in Beacon Bluff—roots she'd finally planted on her own terms. If he'd asked her to leave, to follow him, he'd be no better than her late husband—the man who'd molded her to fit his idea of a perfect life, a perfect wife.

Arden had spent years with her spirit boxed in, her voice barely above a whisper. He couldn't be the reason she lost herself again. But walking away felt like carving something vital from his own chest.

And if he gave in, if he nurtured the love between them the way he wanted, it could only lead to a marriage that withered over time. Arden would shrink, bit by bit, until there was nothing left of the woman he loved.

He couldn't do that—especially now that she was laughing freely and immersing herself in projects she cared about. She was making her own way, after a lifetime of making way for others.

Ending things had to happen for both of them. That's what he kept telling himself. But it didn't explain why he felt like a man who'd just walked away from the one thing that made him whole.

He would focus on the task God had set before him without the distraction of worrying about someone else's happiness. There was much work to do. He had been gone from Honduras for over a year while he raised funding, planned the clinic logistics, and generally worked the stateside aspect of his business plan. Now that he would be on site, he needed to hit the ground running, renewing relationships, and building the clinic.

How he wished Arden could be there to help. He had loved every minute of working side-by-side with her, turning her lighthouse into something she could be proud of. She was a hard worker and an instinctive businesswoman. Hadn't she given him the solution to his clinic store front issues? At her suggestion, he had empowered Don Carlos to hammer out a deal beneficial to the village and Vets Without Boundaries.

Who was he kidding? He missed more than her business sense. He missed her smile and the way her eyes laughed. He missed her encouragement. He missed how she gave him a sense of home that he'd never had before.

He even missed Jonah.

Rubbing his hand across his chest, he hoped to wipe away his heartache. Nick prayed God would help him focus on the greater plan He had for his life. To help him see his way clear from this pain.

Then the older man's words echoed louder than the safety instructions he was supposed to be paying attention to.

*"It is not good for man to be alone."*

Nick's mind finished the biblical quote, *"I will make a helper suitable for you."*

Not wishing for anyone to notice the tears gathering at the edges of his eyes, Nick focused on the scenery outside the window. He didn't envy the relationship between his seat mates. Not quite. It was more...recognition.

The steady kind of love, the kind that knew your faults and loved you anyway. And walking away from it? Maybe that wasn't strength. Maybe it was fear wearing a noble mask.

It was like scales had fallen from his eyes. Nick finally saw his fear for what it was—a deep, gnawing dread that a life of ministry wouldn't be enough to keep Arden happy. Just like it hadn't been enough for his mom. And if Arden wasn't happy...she might be the one to walk away.

He'd be alone. Again.

Unfortunately, this epiphany didn't come with detailed instructions. While he finally understood God didn't mean for Arden and Honduras to be an either/or situation, he didn't understand how to blend the two. He needed to tend to what he started in Honduras. But after that?

The wife touched his arm and tipped her head toward the flight attendant.

Nick removed an earbud to hear better.

"Would you care for a beverage?"

Nick smiled. "I'll take a Diet Coke."

## CHAPTER 21

rden stood in her kitchen, disconnected the call, and did a little shimmy. She had booked the last room through the end of October and had some folks on a waiting list. Her first guests would arrive in one month's time and Keeper's Quarters would be off and running from there.

Having the Faith Works gala in Beacon Bluff had given her place more exposure than if she had taken out an ad in Times Square. Word of mouth had spread, and now her dream had become reality.

Now was the time for Phase Two of her master plan.

Her smile turned wistful. It had been a month since the gala. While God had been gracious in His comfort, she still missed Nick terribly. While she was happy he received his funding, Arden wished he were here. She caught herself wanting to ask his opinion on a particular project or looking for him when she entered a room.

Jonah trotted into the kitchen, dragging an old T-shirt Nick had left behind.

The day after Nick had left for Honduras, Jonah had found it and drug it to bed.

181

They had both slept with it, no matter how desperate or pathetic she felt. Nick's lingering scent had chased away her insomnia.

Arden rushed out to the lighthouse to share the latest good news with her mom.

After the gala, Mom had sent Dad back to Honduras without her, canceling or postponing her existing commitments. "I've just now got you back. I'm not going anywhere."

Arden had dutifully protested, but secretly, she cherished this time with her mom.

Mom was on the third level, admiring their handiwork. She had been applying the final touches to the stencil they had applied to the concrete floor.

Arden joined her, putting an arm around her mom's waist. "This mandala is gorgeous. It's so much better than a rug that would grow mold, and the intricate design hides the flaws in the concrete. I think the docents will enjoy their new break room."

Standing to admire their handiwork, her mom agreed. "We make a good team, don't we?"

"We do." She shared her booking news, and she and her mom hugged each other, jumping up and down like two teenagers at a Taylor Swift concert.

When they regained their composure, Arden asked, "Do you think you can hold down the fort for a few days?"

Her mother cocked an eyebrow. "What did you have in mind?"

Arden grinned. "It's time I head to Honduras, don't you think?"

NICK WATCHED his best friend approach. The guest cottage on the H3 campus had been home since he arrived in Honduras a month ago. He may not have seen Colin since the gala, but Nick knew what lay in store.

Nick opened the screen door and met Colin on the porch. May as well take this outside. No sense breaking the furniture.

Colin kept advancing until he was nose-to-nose with Nick—an MMA fighter about to square up.

Opting for a humorous approach, Nick said, "I don't suppose distance has made your heart grow fonder."

Colin narrowed his eyes. "I warned you."

The tension was so sharp, Colin could have used it as a blade against him.

Nick stepped back, holding his arms out to the side. "Go ahead. I won't stop you."

Colin shoved him against the house, then pulled himself back. "Unfortunately, she made me promise not to hurt you." He turned away with a look of disgust, running his hands through his hair. "Why she'd want to protect you is beyond me."

Nick snorted. "You and me both." He straightened and sat beside his friend on the porch step. "If it makes you feel any better, this past month without her has punished me far more than anything you could do to me."

"It doesn't, and I doubt it."

Nick contemplated the distant mountains. Talking about feelings with another guy went against the laws of nature. But if he hoped for any reconciliation with Arden, he had to make peace with her brother. Besides, he would do whatever was necessary to not lose his best friend.

"Colin, every time I close my eyes, I see her just as I left her. Crying at the top of her lighthouse." He dropped his head between his shoulders. "It's killing me. I spend my days as a healer, yet I managed to hurt the most important person in my world. The woman I love."

Wind blew through the trees, sun beat down on their heads, insects buzzed in the nearby garden. Eventually, tension gave way to brotherhood remembered.

Colin took a deep breath and let it out. "About time you came to your senses. What are you going to do about it?"

"I'm going after her." Like duh.

That got Colin's attention. "Really? If you're messing with me, my sister will not be able to hold me back."

"See for yourself." He nodded back to the screen door. I was packing my bags before you got here."

Colin's narrowed eyes expressed his mistrust. "As I understand, you're living here and she's living there. What's changed since the last time you saw her?"

"I'm not going to tell you before I tell her. Let's just say that God has impressed upon me the importance of flexibility."

Colin stood and turned toward Nick with the first hint of a smile. "Don't screw this up. Monroe."

Nick clapped him on the shoulder before heading back inside to finish packing. "That's the plan."

~

"LADIES AND GENTLEMEN, we have begun our descent into San Pedro Sula. Please stay seated with your seat belts fastened and return your trays to their upright position."

Arden glanced out the window, admiring the lush, rugged mountains below. How could she have waited so long to return?

Honduras was a country full of vibrant colors, abundant natural resources such as waterfalls and even a barrier reef. But most importantly, the beauty of the country was reflected in the warmth and friendliness of its people.

After retrieving her suitcase from customs, Arden stepped into the open area, searching through the crowd for Colin. She didn't see him, so she stepped outside to the loading area and looked for the H3 van.

She frowned. Not there. A text message dinged, so she dug out her phone:

Meet me at the Delta ticket counter.

What was Colin doing there? Maybe he had to drop someone off at the airport. Still, why wasn't the van out front?

Weary from travel, she dragged her suitcase to the other side of the small airport, dodging the crowd. This was so annoying. They still had a two-hour drive to Pena Blanca, and she wanted to see Nick. Now that they shared the same soil, she was impatient to lay eyes on him again.

Impatience was only one of the feelings swirling around her stomach. Fear was another. What if she had traveled 2,782 miles, only to be heartbroken once more?

She had wrestled with God for the past month, and He had convinced her that her past was no indication of her future. He could change the script. But she needed to take the step of faith.

She had gripped her past so tightly, her hands had been fisted against His blessings. The blessing of a loving family, the blessing of a man who loved her. She was so busy looking in the rearview mirror, she couldn't see what God was placing in front of her.

Now, with her vision cleared from hurt and fear, she didn't need to wrestle so hard for her future. God had filled her with a peace that passed all human understanding—her parents weren't the enemy and neither was H3.

Late night talks with her mom had helped Arden develop a plan that would combine her love for Beacon Bluff with the love for her family.

Mom had been right. Beacon Bluff and Honduras didn't need to be an either/or proposition. She had her compromise in mind, now it was up to Nick.

And even if things didn't work with Nick, Arden was excited to partner with her mom and advance H3's women's ministry. Together they had devised a plan where she could make a meaningful difference in Honduran women's lives while maintaining a home base in Beacon Bluff.

But how perfect would it be if things with Nick did work out?

This time, she would not latch on to a man's life, hoping to make it her own. If she hoped to stitch together any semblance of a life with Nick, it wouldn't be at the expense of her own identity.

God had created her to shine, and she couldn't do that beneath any man's shadow. Not even Nick's.

Arden searched the Delta ticketing area, looking for her brother's tall frame. Her gaze swung from left to right. Then it froze. She looked back to the left. Was that? No. It couldn't be.

Breath stuck in her throat as she pushed her way toward the man who caught her eye. She had never been so thrilled to see an orange baseball hat. Bless Colin's heart and his interfering instincts.

"Nick."

She thought she'd breathed his name, but his head jerked up and he looked around.

His gaze locked with hers and it was like they were in an old-time movie, when the couple move toward each other in a field of wildflowers.

Against her better judgment, she left her luggage unattended and ran to Nick.

He met her halfway, dropped his duffel bag and grabbed her in his arms, swinging her in a wide circle.

Arden registered a smattering of applause from onlookers, but she didn't care.

Nick set her down and ushered her back to her suitcase.

He tossed aside his hat and gently grabbed her face, kissing her as if she were drowning and needed the kiss of life.

And she did. His was the kiss of her life.

She ran her fingers through his hair. "Don't ever get rid of that hat. It's how I found you. Twice."

He pulled back, his gaze raking across her face as if to convince himself she was real. "What are you doing here? I was coming to see you."

"You were? It seems I beat you to it." She grinned, unable to stop smiling. She looped her arms about his neck and pulled his head back down. "One more kiss. Then we'll talk."

"At your service."

This kiss was gentle, a balm to their battered souls. His lips lightly brushed back and forth against hers before sinking into the softness. She poured every ounce of feeling into the embrace. Her Nick.

But for how long?

Disentangling herself from the embrace, she reached out and grabbed his hand, using her other to pull her suitcase. "Come on. I see a free bench."

They sat angled toward one another, fingers tangled. For several heartbeats, they just stared at each other.

Arden swallowed. "Why were you coming to see me?"

Nick reached out and brushed her cheek. "So many reasons, and I can't think of a single one right now. I just know I love you, and I couldn't stay away any longer."

Bright light infused her insides. Would disappointment extinguish it? Or would it be fanned even brighter by answered prayer? Now was the time to find out.

He tucked an ever-rebellious curl behind her ear. "What about you? Why are you in Honduras, of all places?"

"I love you too. So much. I'm here to fight for us, Nick. I'm here to face you down and make you consider a future for us. No more running off without talking." She paused and smacked him on the shoulder. "I'm still mad at you for that."

He hugged her tight, resting his chin on the top of her head. "You should be. I'm still mad at myself." He set her aside, holding onto her shoulders so he could look her in the eye. "God has worked inside me in a big way, Arden. I'm so sorry for letting fear of losing you become a self-fulfilling prophecy. We have details to work out, but we belong together, Arden. From the moment I rescued your little dog, I was a goner."

"About those details... I'd like to open the negotiations."

Nick settled himself against the bench, tucking her beneath his arm. "Let's hear what you got."

"I'll go into specifics later, but I've made peace with my parents and H3. I let hurt isolate me for far too long. From my family and from you."

Nick grasped her hand and brought it to his lips.

She almost lost her train of thought. She cleared her throat and continued. "Mom showed me some amazing jewelry some of the women had made for her. We bounced ideas back and forth, and I've decided to work with her contacts and identify artisans who need to put food on their tables. And now that Keeper's Quarters is on solid footing—I'll tell you about that later—I'm going to open a shop in Beacon Buff to sell what they make. All the proceeds will go back to them. If all goes well, we'll expand into an online store."

Nick said nothing. He just gazed at her with a look she couldn't describe. "So, you'll still live in Beacon Bluff? I assume you'll need to make occasional trips back to Honduras. Is that your solution to our situation?"

Her excitement sank like a rock in the pit of her stomach. "Nick, I can't do all the work here. I need a counteroffer from you if we're ever to work this out."

He broke into a smile. "You're in luck. I happen to have one. It was actually your idea."

The smile gave her hope. "What do you mean?"

"Remember when you suggested I should have local residents be front men for the ministry?"

"Yes, but I was only referring to renting space for the clinic."

"It was such a novel idea, I expanded on it. I've been working with *Universidad Nacionale de Agricultura*, Honduras' vet school. I've identified five Honduran vets who are interested in joining Vets Without Boundaries. They're excited to follow our model of opening regional clinics and sharing God's love along with providing animal care."

"I'm confused. How does this get us living in the same country?"

"While I'll want to keep my hands on treating some animals, by and large, I'll play an administrative role. A role I can eventually perform anywhere with cell service and internet access."

"Even a lighthouse on the coast of North Carolina?" Happiness, hope, fear...it was a regular wrestling match in her stomach.

"That thought has crossed my mind." He rubbed his thumb along her jaw. "I've missed Beacon Bluff almost as much as I've missed you. I didn't know being part of a community could feel so good. Now that I do, I want to become part of it. And I believe God agrees."

She tucked herself closer, under his arm. "I'm so glad, Nick. Beacon Bluff has missed you as well." She chuckled. "Even Bea and Miss Ivey."

"I will have to make several trips a year to Honduras. And I'll want you with me."

"Lucky for you, that fits into my retail business plan. I'll have to make several buying trips myself."

She tilted her head, gave him a prim and proper look, and held out her hand. "It seems we have the beginning of an agreement. Shall we shake on it?"

"I have a better idea." Nick's nose rubbed hers.

"I like the way you do business," she whispered against his mouth.

Nick broke away and kneeled before her.

Her gasp was so loud it bounced off the cinderblock walls. "What are you doing?" Arden's hand flew to cover her mouth, her eyes about to pop out of her head.

"Arden Bennett Gray, I know we have a lot of logistics to work out. But I'm committing to spend the rest of my life with you. Will you marry me?"

"Have you asked Jonah for his blessing?"

He rolled his eyes, still on one knee. "Seriously, Arden? Jokes?"

She fell to her knees in front of him. "I intend to spend the rest of my life laughing with you, Nick Monroe. Why not start now?"

He tipped her chin toward him, seriousness replacing every speck of humor. "Is that a yes?"

"It is."

They stayed on their knees, hugging each other for who knew how long, ignoring the people rushing to get to wherever they were going. As for Arden, she was right where she belonged.

Nick stood, grabbing his hat and their bags. "Come on, I can't wait to tell Colin the news. Maybe now I won't have to sleep with one eye open." He bent for a quick kiss. "Let's head back to Pena Blanca."

Arden laughed, tucking her hand into his arm. "To Honduras and beyond."

∼

The towering cylinder of the Beacon Bluff Lighthouse rose behind them as Nick and Arden posed for one of a gazillion wedding photos.

Arden held Jonah, who looked dapper in his tuxedo, including the bow tie and button cuffs. Their pup assumed an air of importance—taking credit for the festivities of the day. Which was only fitting since he had introduced them.

Nick moved behind her, wearing a tux of his own. He wrapped his arms around her from behind and she leaned into his warmth.

It was mid-May, fifteen months since that epic day in the Honduras airport. Just as they had put on a show for the San Pedro Sula travelers, Beacon Bluff was putting on a show for the wedding guests—Carolina blue skies, eighty-degree soft breezes, and a riot of blooming color.

"You look beautiful, Mrs. Monroe."

She tipped her head back against her husband's shoulder and smiled. "Say it again."

"You look beautiful?" She elbowed him in the stomach.

His lips lowered to her ear, brushing them with his breath.

"Mrs. Monroe." The gravel in his voice scraped against her spine. "Better?"

Arden registered the distant click of camera phones and the professional photographer's Nikon, but her eyes and ears were only for Nick. "Much better."

Bea stepped up and exchanged Jonah for the bridal bouquet of white roses and baby's breath.

Even though this was Arden's second wedding, she was outfitted completely in white. God had gifted her with this fresh beginning, and she wanted to celebrate it as such. Her dress had a satin spaghetti strap bodice with a straight, layered tulle skirt. She especially loved the rhinestone encrusted belt around her waist. It was almost as sparkly as she felt on the inside.

She had tossed aside her strappy sandals and now went barefoot, never one to make the same mistake twice.

Nick brushed his nose against her temple. "Thank you for wearing your hair down today.

"I'm not sure how bridal this mess will look in the pictures, but for you, anything."

Tiffany had helped her pull the sides back and anchored it at the crown of her head with a rhinestone clip.

For all her days, Arden would never forget the feel of Nick caressing her neck beneath the heavy curtain of curls when it had been time to kiss his bride.

Nick stepped beside her and put his arm around her waist. "Let's go greet everyone." He led her to where most guests stood with flutes of non-alcoholic champagne, watching as the photographer captured memories that Arden would relive time after time.

They came to a stop and the crowd gathered around. Arden hadn't wanted a circus event like the first time, so she and Nick had only invited family and those who had been part of their story.

Nick took the glass Colin handed him and cleared his throat.

"I know it's not traditional for the groom to offer the first toast, but I have no idea what my best man will say, so I'm saying my piece first."

Everyone laughed, and Colin acknowledged the dig with a raised glass.

Once it was quiet again, Nick continued. "First and foremost, we wish to thank you all for joining with us to celebrate our special day. The occasion wouldn't be complete if you weren't here."

He squeezed Arden's waist, signaling her turn. "Bea and Miss Ivey, what can we say? You've been in my life since I was knee high to a seagull, and you had my back until Nick earned your approval."

"That's right, girl. And we always will." Bea threw a mock scowl at Nick to keep him on his toes.

More laughter.

Then Nick continued. "John. Lila. You've raised a strong, faith-filled daughter who delights my soul each day. And for that, I will be forever in your debt." The thickness in Nick's voice, and the love in his eyes when he looked at Arden, threatened every woman's eye makeup and challenged every man's resolve to not cry in public.

Arden's mother blew a soft kiss towards Nick, her hands clasped above her heart. Dad dipped his head.

Arden cleared her throat and turned toward Nick's parents. "Herb and Louise. Thank you for raising the man of my dreams."

Louise wept happy tears into her handkerchief and Herb all but vibrated with pride.

Colin threw up his hands, interrupting the intermittent sniffs and loud sighs. "How am I supposed to follow an act like that? Now I need to wait until everyone's recovered before offering my roast—er, toast."

"Arden! Nick! Come quick! It's Jonah!" Miss Ivey never raised her voice. Ever. Yet everyone at the wedding reception heard her.

Arden dropped her bouquet, hiked her skirts, and took off running toward the beach, Nick right behind her. When she stopped on a dime, he ran into her back, catching her before they fell.

"Look. He's swimming." Arden's voice was hushed, afraid to scatter the moment.

Jonah was paddling as fast as his little legs could churn. He clamped a piece of driftwood in his mouth, the prize that had lured him into taking the plunge. He was heading for shore, the gentle surf urging him along.

Colin pushed his way through the guests, shoes off and tux pants rolled to the knees. He waded into the water, grabbed Jonah and brought him out. "Ugh. Wet dog." He held Jonah away from his body, tiny dachshund legs dangling, doggy tuxedo utterly ruined.

Stella ran toward Colin and wrapped Jonah with a spare tablecloth she must have nabbed from the caterer. "I got him."

Their friends returned to the reception, but Colin hung back. He unrolled his pant legs and carried his shoes to where Arden stood. Nick was shaking hands with his dad.

Colin squeezed her hand. "Den, you look beautiful. But mostly, you look happy. I regret ever having doubted you."

She grasped his hand and kissed him on the cheek. "Thank you. I hope someday you find the one you're meant to be with."

He grinned, but Arden saw shadows flit across his eyes. "Nah. You and Nick got the whole romance thing covered. I'm good." He kissed her forehead, turned her shoulders, nudging her toward Nick. "Quit wasting your time talking with me when you could be beside your husband."

Arden glanced over her shoulder and winked. "If you insist."

Despite her teasing words, she relished moving toward Nick and claiming the crook of his elbow.

Arden turned in Nick's embrace, tilting her head to meet his gaze. "Can you believe Jonah jumped into the ocean? Looks like he found his happy ending as well."

Nick kissed her lips, lingering for just a moment. "#Arick for life."

**Not ready to leave Beacon Bluff just yet?**
Honestly… neither am I.

I've got a bonus scene from *Finding Jonah* waiting for you—because some moments (and some dachshunds) deserve a little more page time.

***Finding Jonah Bonus Scene***

# WHAT'S NEXT?

## PRODIGAL DAD - BEACON BLUFF BOOK 2

*Don't Miss Book 2 in the Beacon Bluff Series*

*Colin didn't expect to fall for the woman raising his son— and Tessa didn't expect to let him.*

*Begin Reading Prodigal Dad*

# ACKNOWLEDGMENTS

This is a tough one. As a debut author, I've dreamed of getting to write my own Acknowledgment page. But now that I'm here… I'm overwhelmed. There are so many, many people who have contributed to this book's existence. Please know, if you aren't represented here, it's not because your impact wasn't important. It just means that there are so many to list and I'm terrified of leaving someone unacknowledged.

My writing journey has taken many, many—way too many—years for me to reach this milestone. It started the very first time I picked up a book as a child. And it's not over.

First and foremost, praise be to God who not only gifted me with whatever abilities I might have, but also for the patience in waiting for me to get with the plan. I would be nowhere in life without Him.

Thank you to so many writing professionals who cheered for me and came alongside me as I battled through this process of writing a book. Critique partners, beta readers, book coach, editors, cover designers, conference speakers…the list continues. Thank you from the bottom of my heart.

And my family. What can I say? They've put up with my hand-wringing, self-doubts, and tunnel vision when I was in the "zone." They've listened to conversations between me and my characters and pretended I wasn't crazy. Billy, my very own stalwart support. Brosnan and Aeris, my new adult kids that keep me current on trends, lingo, and any cringe-worthy moments. (Any errors in that department are purely my own.) Love you three the most.

And you, my reader. (Yikes! I have readers! Pinch me!) I'm humbled that you read about these imaginary friends inside my head. I pray they've blessed you as much as they've blessed me.

# ABOUT THE AUTHOR

## DENISE GORE LONG

Blame it on Ned Nickerson, Nancy Drew's loyal and oh-so-swoony boyfriend. Like most writers, I began my career through a love of books. As a young girl, my parents would bribe me (though they preferred *reward*) with a Nancy Drew novel to add to my growing library. While the intrepid teenage sleuth kept me on the edge of my seat, it was Ned who made me sit up straight.

It was only natural that I'd evolve into a romance author. I handwrote my first book at fifteen, sequestered for the summer in our finished basement. I turned it into a veritable writer's nest and hunkered down to unleash my muse. I often wonder what happened to that first effort, but I remember it captured all my teenage angst—and a highly theoretical view of true love.

Now, many—so many—years and life experiences later, I've returned to my love of writing. My process has evolved from pen and paper to a keyboard and backup systems, but I still believe in hope, healing, and happily-ever-afters.

One last thing. My stories may be fiction, but my dependence on Diet Coke is very, very real.

www.ingramcontent.com/pod-product-compliance
Lightning Source LLC
Chambersburg PA
CBHW060318310726
48976CB00007B/2376